'In this novel Mary We[...] a
victim of all four categ[...] is
happening to him, wit[...] lf.
She crafts into the story some of the ways that [...]ns
of abuse deal with the pain, but this isn't a novel that delves
into the darkness of abuse, but a story of hope and learning
to trust again. On his journey, Tiago finds people across the
age and social spectrum who could hurt him or could help
him. He has to decide if he will trust again. Are the gang of
runaways going to be like the bullies at school or will their
shared experience bring a level of understanding? Can he
trust the gypsies or are the stereotypes of them true? Who
is he? What worth does he have? Can he trust anyone?
Does he belong anywhere and what does family really
mean?

'Tiago discovers he has a value and can be loved as a
friend, as a brother, as a son and as a boyfriend; that real
love is not conditional or self-serving, but sacrificial and
unconditional; that if you are being abused there are
people whom you can trust and who will help you –
because it's not right and you don't have to live with it.'
*Mark Blackwell, Safeguarding Advisor, Hampshire County
Council*

the runaway

Mary Weeks Millard

instant
ap stle

First published in Great Britain in 2019

Instant Apostle
The Barn
1 Watford House Lane
Watford
Herts
WD17 1BJ

British Library Cataloguing-in-Publication Data

A catalogue record for this book is available from the British Library

This book and all other Instant Apostle books are available from Instant Apostle:

Website: www.instantapostle.com

E-mail: info@instantapostle.com

ISBN 978-1-912726-01-1

Printed in Great Britain

author's note

The characters and situations in this book are entirely a work of fiction and bear no relation to any real person or actual happening, although the story is set in real locations.

dedication

For Daniel, one amazing teenager who has encouraged
me to keep on writing stories.

acknowledgements

My grateful thanks to Mark Blackwell, safeguarding advisor within Hampshire County Council, for taking time to pre-read this book and giving helpful advice and encouragement.

Many thanks, too, to Miss Cathie Smith who, as a former foster mother of a troubled teenager, was willing to read and give advice.

My thanks as ever must go to my ever-patient and loving husband, Malcolm, who encourages me to continue writing and supports me in so many ways.

My thanks, too, to the team at Instant Apostle publishing house for their input and work.

chapter one

Tiago Costa's mouth was beginning to go dry, his heartbeat was racing and his hands shaking as the clock on the wall showed 3.20pm. Already his mind had switched off from the French lesson which Mademoiselle Le Bon was teaching, and he was planning his escape route from the school building. It was imperative that he escaped the clutches of the gang of school bullies; he must outwit them.

Tiago knew he was fair game for the bullies. He was short – his Portuguese heritage had made sure of that – his dark hair stuck up like spikes all over the place and, worst of all, his face sported loads of zits!

'If only I was good at something,' he thought to himself, 'something which could make me popular – especially some kind of sport – they might leave me alone.'

But at best he knew he was only 'average' – or so the school reports said. Then, to make things even worse, his clothes were awful! They were old, not washed as frequently as he would have liked, and mostly bought from the local charity shop. No designer labels for him! No wonder he was bullied. It had been like that ever since he started school, and he had never really had a good friend.

Tiago sighed. 'How I wish I had a mate and we could share things, hang out together and stick up for each other.'

There was just one person in his tutor group who gave him a smile from time to time: a girl named Zoe-Ann. Sometimes she even sat with him in the canteen and chatted. Tiago didn't know why she bothered, she had lots of other friends and was very pretty, but it was so cool when she sat with him. Truth be told, he really fancied her!

At last the bell rang to announce the end of the school day, and with a rush of adrenaline pumping through his veins, Tiago was the first to grab his few belongings and dash to the locker rooms to collect his school bag. He had to get out – he must escape. Sometimes the rhyme he had heard so often when he was very small and attending pre-school ran through his mind: 'Run, run, as fast as you can! You can't catch me. I'm the gingerbread man!' Every single school day he tried to outwit the bullies and be the first out of the school gates so that he could then run through a couple of streets and merge into the general hubbub of Upper Street, Islington. It wasn't until he reached there that he felt even remotely safe. But he still kept looking behind him every few minutes, scared that they might be catching him up.

It had become a horrible sort of game for him, trying to outwit the bullies every single day, before school, at school, but most of all, after school and to get home safely without being attacked. The adrenaline rush somehow enabled his wobbly legs to run faster than he could ever run on the sports field. His greatest fear was that he might be stabbed – he knew some of the guys carried knives.

It was dark and murky that November day, but Tiago decided to go through the street market. It was bustling and noisy with loads of people around. He knew it inside out, and could dodge around the stalls, because at weekends and school holidays he worked on a fruit and vegetable stall, and considered Tom, the owner, and his wife, Val, his only real friends.

'Look who it ain't, Val,' said Tom, in his booming voice, which he usually used to attract customers to his stall, looking up and smiling at Tiago. 'I'm right glad to see yer, son,' he added. 'Got time for a bit of extra work before you get off 'ome? Our Val needs to visit the doctor – I was 'oping you might come this way and give me a hand while she 'as 'er appointment.'

'I can stay for an hour, Tom, but that's all. I need to get home to get our Lizzie her tea. Mum's not usually up to doing it these days.'

'Thanks, ducks,' said Val, taking off her apron and buttoning up her coat. She grabbed her large handbag and gave Tom a quick peck on the cheek before disappearing through the market stalls to the doctor's surgery.

''Ow is your Lizzie, then?' asked Tom. 'It's bin a while since we've seen 'er.'

'I know, and sorry about that,' answered Tiago. 'It's easier in the holidays to bring her out. Mum is glad when I do that. It's good for her to get fresh air.'

Tiago rarely talked about his life at home, but Tom and Val had a pretty good idea that things were miserable for him and his two-year-old sister, Lizzie. Val loved to cuddle

15

Lizzie when Tiago brought her down to the market. Her experience told her that the two kids were neglected. They wore clothes that were well past their best, their hair needed cutting and their shoes were scuffed; but that was typical of many of the kids who lived in that part of Islington. Sometimes Val brought Lizzie a toy or a nice dress from another stall, but she rarely saw the things again, so she guessed that the children's mother had problems and probably sold the items for cash. Tiago was very loyal and only ever hinted that his mum was ill and not able to cope.

'I have to get going now,' said Tiago, at the end of the hour. Tom gave him a hefty tip and a bag of fruit to take home with him.

'Thanks again, mate,' he said to the lad. 'See you on Saturday morning, nice and early, to set up the stall.'

'Sure thing,' answered Tiago, happy for a bit more money to add to his secret stash of savings. Sometimes he was tempted to buy a decent T-shirt with a logo on it, or a nice pair of trainers, but he was saving up every penny from his work in the market and his early morning paper round. One day soon he planned to run away from all his troubles and knew he would need money and equipment. He had a place in the garden shed where he kept his savings – it was safer than indoors where his mum or her boyfriend might find and steal it, then spend it all on drink or drugs.

chapter two

Tiago ran back through the streets – always on the lookout for the gang of bullies. Fear gave him flight once again as he ran down one street and up the next. They all looked much the same, rows of Victorian terraced houses; many of them, like the one where he lived, needing a lick of paint.

As he came to the end of the road he could see that his mother's boyfriend, Jack, was home, because he had parked his lorry outside. The very sight of it made Tiago feel sick. As he neared the house, he went up the side alley and quietly unlatched the back gate (or as quietly as he could because it was rusty and squeaked as he pushed it open). He put his hand into his trouser pocket and felt for his key to the padlock on the shed door. No one else ever went to the shed, but he had bought a strong padlock for himself, just to make sure his money would be safe. He hid his wages under several flowerpots. Tiago knew that it would be safer in the post office or a bank, but there was nothing he could do about getting an account, so he tried to hide it as best he could and hoped against hope it would be OK.

Behind the shed he had a small vegetable plot. This time of the year there was nothing growing, but during the summer months he managed to grow tomatoes. Once, Tom gave him some squashed tomatoes and he had saved the seeds and planted them. It had been so exciting to see the plants grow, and he had felt so proud of himself for providing some food for the family.

Tiago carefully locked the shed and went up the garden path to the back door, quietly letting himself in. He put the fruit which Tom had given him on the cluttered kitchen table. What a mess the kitchen was. There were dirty dishes in the sink, the floor was stained and the tiles were cracked. Tiago looked around in disgust and wrinkled his nose at the smell. He hated the mess in which they lived and did his best to clean up from time to time, but since no one else cared, his efforts didn't last very long. He sighed deeply. How he wished he could wave a magic wand and things would change – but he knew that didn't happen in real life.

Jack must have heard him come in, for he bellowed, 'Decided to come 'ome from school, then? What time do yer call this? 'Ave you been skiving off with yer mates somewhere? Yer mum and I are waiting for some tea. She don't feel like making anyfink – so you better get to it!'

Tiago walked into the living room. As usual his mum was half-asleep, still in her grubby night clothes. Lizzie toddled over to him, her clothes stained and her nose running. He could smell that her nappy needed changing, too. Anger rose up inside him. Why was everything left to him, as if he were some sort of slave? Lizzie put her arms out and something inside him melted. He picked her up,

18

dodging Jack, who tried to give him a clip around the ear as he crossed the room.

'I'll just see to Lizzie, then I'll see what's in the fridge and cook you something,' he said to Jack, and his mum opened her eyes and gave a sort of smile. She had that 'faraway' look and Tiago knew she was high on drugs again. He couldn't totally hate his mum, she was weak and sick, but he did hate her boyfriend. He was neither a boy nor a friend!

He took Lizzie to the bathroom and tried to wash her sore bottom. He couldn't understand because she was bleeding and bruised; she always had a nappy rash, but there had never been blood there before. A horrible thought came into his mind – had that louse of a man hurt her – tried to abuse her? Wasn't it bad enough that he abused his mother and did unmentionable things to Tiago in the night – but to hurt his own little girl, only two years old? That was unforgiveable! What should he do? What could he do?

Tiago's mind was reeling as he carried her downstairs and took her into the kitchen. He sat her in the playpen. It was like a prison in which she spent most of her daylight hours.

The pain he felt inside was unbelievable. He thought his stomach would burst, but he didn't dare say anything about what he suspected.

'I must focus,' he thought to himself. 'I must cook something – then Jack will go to the pub for a while. Then I can think what to do. I must make a plan.'

There wasn't much food around, but Tiago found some eggs and bread and made toast and an omelette. He made sure that Lizzie had a share before putting his mum and Jack's portions on plates and taking them into the living room, along with mugs of strong tea. There was little left for himself, but Tiago felt too sick at heart to eat. He washed the fruit he'd been given, cut up an apple into small pieces for his sister and put the rest in the fridge. Maybe he'd have some later.

Then he set to work trying to clean up the mess in the kitchen. It was therapeutic, in a strange way. It helped his inner pain when he worked hard, scrubbing and tidying up. It helped his mind to go blank.

Tiago waited until he heard Jack go out, slamming the front door behind him. He heard the lorry engine revving up and moving away. Thank goodness! Now he would have a couple of hours of peace. He went back into the living room and collected the dirty plates and mugs to wash.

'Ta, Ti,' said his mum. 'I feel tired, love – just going up to bed. Get me that bottle, will you?' She pointed to a bottle of cheap plonk that Jack must have brought home for her. 'Can you see to your sister? I'm too tired.'

'You're always too tired,' Tiago grumbled under his breath, then said, 'Yes, Mum,' and walked back into the kitchen. It was always the same these days – his mum was incapable of taking care of her kids, or even herself.

'Come on then, Lizzie,' Tiago spoke gently, picking up his sister and going upstairs. He took her to her cot and saw that the sheet was stained with blood. Anger pulsed through him – he felt like shouting and screaming as hate for Jack filled him. He was sure that Jack had abused his sister. He must do something, he must tell someone, and somehow he and Lizzie had to escape. Tiago changed the stained sheets and tucked up his sister, feeling angry, sad and confused.

'I'll make sure you are alright – somehow I'll protect you, Lizzie, before I leave,' he whispered and gave her a kiss on the cheek, then sang her a nursery rhyme before closing her door.

His next job was to tackle the laundry. Most of the equipment in the house had been sold to pay for his mum's drink and drug habit, but he could still wash the clothes in the old washing machine. He loaded it, then took his torch and went to the shed. That place had become his refuge. Tiago had found a way to help him to cope with his emotional pain. He found that by hurting himself it blotted it out, if only for a short time. He had devised different ways of doing this and the pain he inflicted on himself somehow seemed to alleviate the pain inside him. Sometimes he burnt himself; other times he used a sharp knife to cut his wrist. He didn't cut deeply, as he didn't want to bleed to death, but just injured himself enough to get rid of his inner pain. So far, nobody had noticed his scars or questioned him about them.

Once Tiago felt calmer he began to think. He had to get out of this situation but could not leave without knowing Lizzie would be safe. He probably had enough money saved up to buy the essentials he would need to survive while he found himself somewhere safer to live. Anything had to be better than the living hell his life had become! The only place he felt even remotely happy was at the market with Tom and Val, but that was far too near home for safety. He had to get right away – somewhere where he could not be found.

'Maybe I should go abroad, try to find my father's family,' he told himself.

The more Tiago thought about that, the better the idea seemed. Perhaps he could travel to Portugal and find his grandparents – maybe they would love and help him?

Tiago decided that as soon as he was ready to leave, he would tell Tom and Val about Lizzie and what was really going on at home. He hated to think it would mean betraying his mum, but he knew he would have to do so to make sure his sister was safe. She would be taken into care – but there was no way he was going into care, too. He would escape and make his own way in life; get away from school, home and Islington.

Having made his decision, Tiago returned to the kitchen. The washing was done, so he draped it on a rack to dry. He went up to his room and climbed into bed, pulling the old duvet up around him. He looked at his homework and sighed in despair. It wasn't that he hated school work, but he really couldn't keep up – he had no computer, and it was hard to queue in the public library to get a turn to use one; the after-school homework club wasn't much of an option because the bullies might find him there, and several times in the past they had torn his shirt, blazer and once almost strangled him with his tie. He put his books back into his bag and tried to sleep, but his mind was too alert. He was listening for the noise of the lorry and Jack's return. He gritted his teeth as he heard the door slam and the man's boots on the stairs. He could almost count the minutes as he heard him in the loo, then turning the handle of his bedroom door and coming over to his bed.

'Our time together now, ain't it, Ti?' the man leered, pulling the bedclothes off the boy. 'Waiting for me, were you?' The smell of drink was overpowering and Tiago felt sick. He would never get used to the horror of the man's advances and the sexual things he did to him. He just gritted his teeth and silently endured it all. He had learned long ago that this was the best way – get it over with and then the man would go. When the abuse had first started, he had kicked and screamed, but that had made Jack angry and he had beaten him with his belt.

Once the ordeal was over, Jack left the room, and Tiago curled himself up in a ball, sobbing silently – feeling hate towards Jack and himself; he felt dirty, and guilty that he couldn't stop what was happening to him.

chapter three

That night Tiago slept fitfully. His mind was full of plans of how to make his escape. He knew he needed to think it out very carefully; that way he would be less likely to be caught and put into a council-run home, which he dreaded. There had been a time some years previously when his mother had been found drunk and incapable of caring for him. He'd been around five years old and a social worker had taken him away from home and put him in care. He had been so frightened and didn't understand where his mother had gone; although he had been so young he had vowed he would never go through that again. Tiago worried about Lizzie, but felt that she was so young perhaps someone nice would be asked to foster her and she would have a happy childhood.

Early in the morning he quietly got up, washed and dressed and ran to the paper shop. 'Good morning, Tiago,' said the newsagent. 'Nice dry day for you to do your round.'

'Mr James,' answered Tiago, 'I have to give you a week's notice. I'm afraid I won't be able to do the round any longer.'

'Oh, Tiago, surely you are not going to give it up?' replied Mr James in dismay. 'You're so punctual and reliable and it's hard to get young people who are reliable. What's the problem – can I help at all?'

'I'm afraid I'll be moving away for a while,' replied Tiago, reluctantly. He didn't want to have to answer lots of questions and he hated lying. 'My mum isn't well – but maybe when she's better I'll come back,' he said with a smile, then grabbed his bag of papers and ran out of the shop before Mr James asked any more awkward questions.

'Thank goodness,' he thought. 'That's the first thing done. I just hope he keeps it to himself.' There was a bit of comfort in the fact that the shop was on the main road, quite a distance from where he lived.

Once the round was finished Tiago ran home, grabbed a slice of bread, and then set off for school. He always timed his morning routine very carefully, so that he entered the school gates just before the bell rang, avoiding the playground and the gang of bullies. Today, he felt a real sense of freedom bubbling inside of him. Soon he would be rid of their threats forever; little did they know that he would be free from their tyranny and he would be the winner!

It was Friday morning and Tiago had decided that the best day for him to make his escape would be the following Sunday week. That meant he could work his notice properly and get his wages for the paper round, work two more Saturdays in the market, have time to buy essentials for living rough, and leave when Jack was due to be off on a long-distance run with the lorry.

The following week everything went pretty much to plan. Tiago bought a sleeping bag, blanket and a large backpack. He stored the things safely in his shed. Then he thought about the money he had saved and the best way to carry it safely. He knew some people put money in their socks, but he had too much to do that. In the end, he decided to buy a money belt to wear under his clothes, around his waist. He also bought some needles and thread from a market stall and sewed some of the money into the lining of his jacket. Other small items, like the things which he used to relieve his inner pain, he stowed away in the backpack. He was almost ready! Happiness and an excitement he hadn't felt for years surged through him as he made his plans. He felt that at long last he had some control over his life. He could become somebody – he didn't know who or what – but it had to be better than his present existence; as long as he made sure Lizzie was safe, too.

There was one thing which Tiago still needed to do. Jack had left on Friday afternoon for his long-distance trip, this time driving to Poland. That evening Tiago bought extra food and made a special meal for his mum and Lizzie – mince, veggies and rice. His mum hardly noticed, but he gave her the bottle of wine which was stored in the wardrobe and left her to have her drug fix and then drink the booze. He knew she would soon be 'out for the count'. Once she was unconscious, he made his way to her bedroom. What a mess it was in! However, he had no time to tidy up – he was a man on a mission. Under the bed, covered in dust, was a tin. Years ago, his mum had wanted something from it and sent him to search, so he knew it was full of important documents. Now he was searching to see if he could find his birth certificate. If he were ever to manage to get to Portugal and look for his grandparents, he would need it to obtain a passport.

At the bottom of the tin he found it – but it was folded up inside other documents. Fascinated, he sat and read them. There was a death certificate. He knew his father had died, but he had never been told or even thought to ask any details. 'My dad died at sea; drowned in a fishing accident in 2005. How terrible!' he thought. He thought of the cold seawater filling his dad's lungs and shuddered. No wonder his mum had taken to drink!

The third document he looked at was his parents' marriage certificate. They had been married in a church in Islington in 2001. It gave some facts about his grandfathers. His mother's father, Joseph Harris, had been a gardener, and he was deceased. His father's father was called Frederiko Costa and he was a fisherman. Along with the marriage certificate, Tiago found a black-and-white photo of a couple standing on a bridge. On the back in faint handwriting was 'Emelia and Frederiko Costa, Braga, 1968', and an address written underneath. Tiago stared at the photo of his grandparents. He wondered where Braga was. Did they still live there? He carefully put the photo and three certificates in his pocket, then closed the tin and shoved it back under the bed. A cloud of dust made him sneeze. He took the precious items down to the shed and put them in his backpack to keep them safe, planning to make photocopies of his parents' marriage and his dad's death certificates and to keep his own birth certificate. Tiago had bought a combination lock for the pocket of the backpack, and carefully closed it. He longed to ask his mum about his dad and grandparents, but he knew she might get suspicious. She could be very unpredictable at times, and his main priority was to keep his plan a secret.

Saturday morning found Tiago down at the market as soon as he had made photocopies of the documents at the post office. He was bubbling with excitement and apprehension. Tom soon noticed his young helper was not his usual self.

'Well, Ti,' he said. 'What's going on with you today? Yer excited about somefink. Spill the beans, son.'

'I need to talk to you, Tom – seriously, I mean. When I've finished work today, can I have a talk to you and Val? It's very important, but very, very secret.'

Tom looked at the boy and decided not to press him just now. Whatever the lad had on his mind would keep until the afternoon.

'OK, I'll tell Val to come up and we'll 'ave a natter before yer goes 'ome,' he promised.

The day passed quickly. It was always busy on Saturdays in the market – especially in the morning. So many people were buzzing around. It was colourful and fun. Tiago knew he would miss working there, but he had to leave if his life was to get better. Tom kept looking at him and wondering what was up. He'd grown fond of the lad – he was reliable, trustworthy and a very hard worker, but he'd long ago sussed out the fact that he must have a pretty rough home life – and that poor kid sister of his seemed so neglected.

Val made a brew at the end of the afternoon and when all the customers had gone, Tom called Tiago to come and have a cup of tea. Val also produced a bag of sugary doughnuts, which made his eyes light up.

'Well, spill the beans and tell us what's on yer mind,' Tom told him.

Tiago found it hard to start.

'It's dead secret – you must promise me not to say anything to anybody until Monday,' answered Tiago.

'I promise,' said Tom, and Val nodded, wondering whatever was going on.

Tiago began to tell them the story of his mother and her boyfriend. He struggled to keep his emotions under control and not to cry in front of them as he explained that he was sure Jack was now sexually abusing Lizzie.

'I hate him – he's done horrible things to me, but now he's started on our Lizzie. When I saw that, I knew I had to do something. Please send the social services around on Monday. Not before then – I need time to get away. I'm leaving home forever, but once I'm gone Lizzie will have no one to love her or look out for her.' Tiago handed a piece of paper to Val, on which he had written his home address. 'Please don't tell anyone that I've gone – don't let them catch me or bring me back. Jack threatened to kill me if I split on him, and I know he's capable of doing that.'

Val was crying by now. 'Why don't yer just pick up Lizzie and come to our 'ouse?' she sobbed. 'We'd take care of yer both.'

'He'd find us and kill us, and probably Mum, too,' answered Tiago. 'I have to get far away, never to be found again – out of his clutches forever. But Lizzie must be taken somewhere safe. Don't try to find me. I will try to get to Portugal and find my grandparents.'

Tom and Val were horrified by what they heard, and overwhelmed. Val found a bit of paper and wrote a number on it. ''Ere's Tom's mobile phone number. Call us any time and we'll 'elp yer. We'll go to the social folks first thing on Monday morning. Now, big boy as yer are, give us a 'ug and take care of yerself. Yer a good lad – don't let anyone get yer into bad ways,' she told him.

''Ere's your wages, and a bit of a bonus. Call it a Christmas bonus if yer like. I owe yer – and take care of yerself,' said Tom, handing a wad of notes to Tiago – far, far more than his usual Saturday pay.

'Thanks,' said Tiago, trying not to cry. He had to be in control now; he felt he had to act as a man going out into the world. 'Thanks so much, you've been good friends. That's why I know I can trust you to get help for Lizzie.'

With tears in his eyes he got his jacket and ran away from the market stall, not daring to turn back and wave in case he broke down completely. His life in Islington was over forever; a great adventure and a new start would come in the morning.

chapter four

Tiago was shaking with a mixture of fear and excitement and cold when he got up the next morning. It was very early, still dark outside, but at least it was dry. He dressed carefully, putting on his favourite rugby shirt for warmth, and then his anorak. Carrying his shoes in his hand so as not to make a noise and wake his mum or sister, he made his way to the kitchen. There was enough bread to make himself a jam sandwich, which he put into a bag to take with him, then he put on his shoes and quietly let himself out of the back door. So far, so good! The carefully laid plan was working.

Tiago walked down the garden path to the shed. The first thing he needed to do was to put the money belt securely around his waist. It did bulge rather a lot because he had saved up a considerable sum, but it was safer next to his skin than in his backpack. His backpack felt very heavy when he slid it over his narrow shoulders, but he knew he'd need all the contents. Then he pulled a navy beanie hat as far over his head as possible.

He was ready at last! The rhyme went through his mind again, like a mantra: 'Run, run, as fast as you can! You can't catch me. I'm the gingerbread man!'

The roads were quiet at that early hour, especially on a Sunday morning. He hoped that nobody would notice him, and silently begged Tom and Val not to grass on him, but to keep his secret until Monday, as they'd promised. It didn't take long to walk through the side roads and into Upper Street, then along to the underground station. Using his London Transport Oyster card, he went through the barrier and down to the platform to catch the first train going north. Tiago tried to be calm, but he found himself listening intently for the rumble of the train and hoping against hope that it would arrive before anyone else came on the platform, in case he was recognised. He was scared of being seen on the CCTV cameras, too, so tried to keep as far away from them as possible.

Tiago was so glad when he saw the snake of the train arrive, and he felt a bit safer once he was inside. He didn't often use the underground because he rarely went anywhere further than he could walk, but he knew the next stop on the line was King's Cross – a major railway station. He got off there and quickly made his way up to the mainline, breathing a sigh of relief when he saw that there were quite a lot of people around and he could mingle with the crowd. Hopefully, nobody would notice him, and he glanced around, searching again for CCTV cameras to avoid being near them. He saw a waiting room on one platform and made a beeline for it, glad to get into a warm room for a while. He told himself that he would have to get used to the cold; running away in November wasn't the best time of year to start sleeping on the streets, but he'd no option. He'd had to make sure Lizzie was safe, and keep his freedom.

Several people in the waiting room were curled up on the seats, asleep. Maybe they were sleeping rough, Tiago thought. Railway stations remained open all night, and they had waiting rooms and toilets. It was a good plan – better than archways, shop door fronts or park benches. He began to feel hungry and his stomach kept rumbling, so he took out his sandwich and ate it quickly. It tasted so good!

For a little while he just sat, trying to plan his next move. Since it was a nice day he decided to explore. On the station forecourt information stand he'd found maps for the underground and buses, as well as one of central London. Looking at these he saw he could easily walk to Regent's Park. Once, when he was small, his mum had taken him there to feed the ducks on the lake. It was one of his few happy childhood memories and he thought it would be fun to go there again.

Tiago left King's Cross and, with the aid of his map, began to walk along Euston Road. He passed Euston Station, crossed the Hampstead Road and walked down Marylebone Road into Regent's Park. He was surprised because there were quite a few people around – some exercising dogs, others jogging and some just walking around. He was on the path which seemed to be on the outer edge of the park when he was startled by a boy on a skateboard. He jumped out of the way as the boy went by at great speed.

'Wow!' thought Tiago. 'That's what I need. A skateboard – why didn't I think about that before? When I find a street market I'll buy one. It'll save my legs no end.' The thought cheered him up and he walked to the edge of the lake and found a seat where he could sit and watch the ducks. They made him laugh and he wished he'd saved a bit of his sandwich for them.

He was about to get up and move on when a guy came and sat by him. 'Hi! You're an early bird, out here on your own on a Sunday morning,' he said jovially.

Tiago was instantly wary. Had this man guessed he was a runaway? He needed to be careful.

'It's not that early. I help at a market but felt like a walk round the park first, today. I like the ducks,' he answered.

'Yeah, me too,' replied the guy. 'I'm Jake. I'm an early bird, too. What's your name?'

'Tim,' answered Tiago, thinking as quickly as he could. 'Tim Cox, pleased to meet you.' He shook the guy's hand before he got up. 'Sorry, mate, but I better get on my way up the road – the market's way past King's Cross. I'd best not be late.'

He started back towards the gate where he had entered the park. He was a bit shaken and the words, 'Run, run, as fast as you can!' ran through his head again. This wasn't going to be as easy as he'd thought. He hated lying but knew that it must become a habit to protect his identity and keep him safe.

'If only I was a bit taller or had some stubble or my voice had really broken, it would be easier,' he thought to himself. 'I don't even look fourteen, let alone being nearly fifteen!'

Once safely out of the park Tiago got out his map and saw that he could easily walk down Great Portland Street and he would be in the West End, in Oxford Street. Time was getting on and the shops would be open. He would feel safer looking around the shops. Maybe he could buy a can of drink and a bun. Tiago's fears melted away a little once he reached Oxford Street. He enjoyed looking around the shops, although his backpack seemed to be getting heavier and heavier. He needed to find somewhere he could sit, so found a fast-food shop, went in and ordered a burger. It tasted good and was a real treat for him.

He felt better once his stomach was full and his back and feet weren't aching quite so much. He continued to explore the West End, and the afternoon passed quite quickly. As soon as the light began to fade, Tiago knew he must decide where he was going to sleep that night. He was feeling cold and very tired, so he consulted his maps and began to make his way to Paddington Station – he'd always loved the Paddington Bear stories when he was a little kid, and it sounded like it could be a friendly place. It was easy enough to get to from Oxford Circus underground station–straight through on the Bakerloo line. When he arrived at Paddington, the mainline station wasn't too busy, so he walked around to get an idea of the layout. No one took any notice of him. Wearing his backpack he blended in with other travellers walking on the forecourt. He soon located a waiting room on platform one and found a seat. His legs were so tired, and his shoulders ached. He pulled from his bag a puzzle book and a pencil, which he had bought earlier in the day, along with a BLT sandwich and a bottle of cola. As the evening wore on Tiago began to feel lonely. A cleaner came in and looked at him suspiciously.

'What train are you catching?' he asked him, and suddenly Tiago felt a bit confused. He had to think quickly. 'I'm waiting for my uncle and then we're going to Bristol – he's getting the tickets,' he lied. He knew his face was going red and from the look he was getting, he knew the cleaner didn't believe him. There were more hazards to running away than he had realised!

When the cleaner had finished, Tiago got up and walked out of the waiting room. He found the coins he needed to get through the turnstile to the loos and went to make himself comfortable. He was cleaning his teeth when a boy came up to him. He appeared to be about the same age and looked at Tiago carefully.

'Are you looking for somewhere to sleep tonight?' he asked. 'A gang of us boys sleep under one of the arches – it's the safest place. What's your name? You're not normally around here, are you?'

Tiago took a deep breath. Could he trust this boy? He looked nice enough and sounded sincere. He decided to take a chance because he just didn't know what he was going to do.

'I'm Tim,' he answered, 'and no, I'm not from around here. Was at King's Cross but decided to try Paddington.'

'Good move, Tim. There are always a lot of transport police around that station, and most of the rough sleepers are older men with dogs. We don't like them. Kids like us are safer here. By the way, I'm Luka,' the boy answered, then continued, 'Been on the road long?' Tiago shook his head. 'I didn't think so – your bag's too new!'

Luka led Tiago to the back of the station. Under a huge arch there was a group of five boys and one very sad-looking girl. Luka introduced Tiago and all the kids seemed quite friendly. It would be nice to belong to a gang, he thought. He'd never had real friends and longed to belong somewhere. Although still wary of the group, Tiago began to smile, trying to learn their names and be friendly.

'We call ourselves the Railway Sleepers' Gang,' Luka explained to him, with a laugh. 'Good name, don't you think? We look out for each other. We get food each night in a church hall. We can trust the guys there – they're straight, and they've never grassed us up. If you're ready, we're about to go. Take everything. Never leave anything down here. Even a cardboard box would get nicked!'

chapter five

Tiago tossed and turned that first night. He was reasonably warm in his sleeping bag and blanket and used his backpack as a pillow – but he was scared. Could he trust these guys? Would they guess he had money around his waist and sewn into his anorak? Would they try to rob him? Did they carry knives? Did they use drugs? They were streetwise, and he knew he wasn't. He would have to get used to being homeless; he couldn't go back now, he had burnt his bridges. He had to somehow forge a new life, but he would need to learn to protect himself.

After the first few days, Tiago began to be less tense and guarded. The gang seemed to like him. He felt proud to belong and started to trust them a little. He even told Luka a bit of why he had run away. The girl, who was called Summer, was listening, and she began to sniffle a bit when she heard about Lizzie. Tiago was sure that she must have run away because of abuse. She was only twelve and he felt quite protective towards her.

During the day, the group dispersed and went their separate ways, coming together as soon as it began to get dark. Tiago used the daytime to explore London – sometimes riding for hours on the underground, sometimes spending hours in museums such as the Natural History Museum. He loved it there. One time there was a school party going around; he found that he could join the crowd and not be noticed, and that way he learned all sorts of things. That was really cool, and he began to enjoy learning new things. He particularly loved learning about plants. It reminded him of his little garden at home – except that it wasn't 'home' any more.

Tiago was very careful with his money, but he did buy food for himself when he was out. He felt a bit guilty that he wasn't sharing his money with the rest of the gang, but it was early days and he still wasn't sure about trusting them completely. He wondered how they got their money, because he knew they did have some. He had also realised that some of the boys were using drugs, and that scared him. His experience at home had taught him enough for him to detest drug usage. He didn't want to be part of that scene.

In the middle of the first week, Luka came up to Tiago.

'The gang go out together sometimes for an adventure. We decided we'll go somewhere tonight. Want to come with us?' he asked.

Tiago was aware it was a kind of test. Would he be loyal to the gang and be trustworthy? Luka wasn't very forthcoming when Tiago asked him what they were going to do.

'We're just visiting a few old churches in the city, Tim. We just see what's about. You'll be surprised what people leave around!' he said with a smile.

Tiago agreed to go. They set off late in the afternoon, in the dusk. The gang all used Oyster cards on public transport and knew the roads well. They had a way of working together; a couple of them hung around a church, while two or three others went inside. Those outside kept watch, while those inside looked for boxes that contained money – and then they robbed them. Luka and Tiago stayed outside most of the time, and Tiago didn't feel too badly about that. Then, at the last stop on the round, he was sent inside with Luka and another lad. As soon as he had entered the church, he felt overwhelmed by the beauty and the peace of the place. It was an amazing feeling. Disregarding the other boys, he went to the front of the church and just gazed around. A noise came from a door near where he was standing, and a man wearing a long, black robe came out. The other boys disappeared in seconds, but Tiago was transfixed, still looking at the beauty around him. The man came up to him and asked if he wanted help.

'Oh no, thanks,' Tiago replied. 'I was just looking at all the beautiful things. It's so peaceful and still and quiet. I've not been in many churches before,' he admitted.

The minister looked at the boy intently and realised he was indeed, awestruck. His first impression had been that he was in the church to cause trouble because he had been warned about a gang of youths who raided churches.

'It's peaceful because God is here,' the minister said quietly. 'You can sit and talk to Him, if you like. I was going to lock up, but I can allow you five minutes.'

'Thanks, mister,' answered Tiago, 'but I don't know how to talk to God.'

'He's like a father,' replied the minister. 'Talk to him like you would your dad.'

'I don't have a dad,' Tiago told him. 'But I'll have a go.' He sat in the pew and closed his eyes. Could this feeling of peace be real?

'Please, God,' he silently prayed, 'You must be real, because I can feel You in here. Take care of Lizzie, give her a good life. Could Mum have some help, too? Please keep me safe on the streets. Thank You for listening.'

Then he got up, said thank you to the minister and walked out of the building. The others were nowhere to be seen, so Tiago retraced his steps to the underground, and he found them there, waiting for him.

'Hey, Tim, thanks. You got us out of trouble there. What did the priest say to you? You must have convinced him you were a good guy doing good things in his church,' Luka said.

'It was OK,' Tiago said, not wanting to tell them how he'd felt in the church and that he could never steal from one. It would be like stealing from God.

Tiago desperately longed to stay with the gang, but he couldn't do what they were doing. He felt very mixed up.

chapter six

During the next few days Tiago began to feel less anxious and more settled. He felt accepted by the Railway Sleepers' Gang, and it was so good to belong to a group and be popular. It was a novel experience – he'd never been popular in his whole life. His new friends seemed to think he was a hero, having allowed them to escape from the church unscathed. He didn't bother to explain that he had been awestruck by the beauty and the peace of the place and had no intention of being part of the robbery!

'If I'm part of this gang, you have to understand one thing – there's no way I'll do drugs! One of the reasons I'm homeless is because drugs ruined our family life. I don't want to go down that road,' Tiago felt bold enough to tell them firmly, even though inside he didn't feel very bold. For the time being, it seemed the gang accepted that.

During the hours of daylight he still did his own thing, as most of the gang did. Luka had become his closest friend, but he also often chatted to Summer. He hated to see her always looking so sad.

'What do you do all day?' she asked one evening.

'I like to visit the free museums and find out about things,' he told her. 'It's fun exploring London. You could come with me sometimes, if you like.'

'No way,' she answered. 'I hated school. But thanks for inviting me.'

'So, what do you do all day?' he asked her.

'I hang around the shops. I look at clothes I could never afford to buy, but sometimes try them on and the feel and look of them makes me feel good. Mostly, I just feel rubbish. The shop assistants look at me as if I'm a lump of dirt someone has brought in on their shoes.'

Tiago felt so sorry for her. 'I hope things get better for you,' he said quietly, 'and for all of us.'

Sadly, things didn't get better for Tiago. Suddenly there was a change in the weather, and as December arrived, so did a very cold spell, even snow. The north-east wind whistled through the arch where the gang were sleeping, and they huddled together to try to keep warm. Summer was so thin, and her clothes were very old. One night, Tiago gave her his spare sweatshirt – it wasn't that good, but he knew he could buy another if he needed one. He felt so sorry for her and hoped that Lizzie would never end up on the streets.

During the cold spell there seemed to be more police patrols around. The gang always tried to make themselves scarce when they saw the cops – all of them were still minors and could be picked up and taken to their homes or to a children's home, and none of them wanted that. They had very sad histories and living on the streets had become a better option for them.

Another thing which happened was the appearance of Zoe-Ann, the girl who had been kind to Tiago in school. He just couldn't believe his eyes one Friday afternoon as he returned to Paddington after spending the day around London. He couldn't take his eyes off her when he saw her wandering around the station, looking at people sitting on the seats and hanging around the waiting rooms. He longed to run over to her, but also began to shake with fear in case his cover had been blown. When she eventually spotted Tiago, she ran over to him with a look of relief on her face. He was glad that none of the gang were around when she called out to him.

'Tiago, thank God I've found you.'

'What on earth are you doing here?' he said to her, a little roughly. 'By the way, people now call me Tim Cox.'

'I need to speak to you, Ti,' she answered, 'and I need to get back home before I'm missed, too. Is there somewhere we can talk?'

'Come into the waiting room on platform one,' he said, 'but we must be careful.'

'*We* must be careful – no, it's *you* who needs to be careful,' Zoe-Ann answered, taking a flyer out of her pocket. 'Look at this: the police are searching for you. They came to school,' she went on to explain, 'and told us you were missing and wanted by the police. Your stepfather has made allegations against you about abusing your sister. I knew you would never do that, but since you had disappeared I thought I must try to find you and warn you.'

'Oh, Zoe-Ann,' Tiago whispered, 'if only you knew the whole terrible story. He's not my stepfather, just my mother's boyfriend. He's done terrible things to both of us and threatened to kill me if I ever told anyone. I had to run away. I had no choice.'

Tiago was now very frightened. He no longer felt safe. Even the gang couldn't help him or hide him from Jack. He began to shake, and his stomach tightened into a knot. He badly needed to hurt himself and get rid of his inner pain.

'How did you know where to find me?' he asked Zoe-Ann, realising that if she had found him so easily, then the police and Jack could do the same.

'Everyone knows there are gangs of runaways at the mainline stations,' she answered. 'I guessed that King's Cross, St Pancras and Euston were too near to home, so thought I would search the others. Today was the first day I could get away without my mother getting worried. I usually go to the library after school on Fridays. Actually,' and at this Zoe-Ann blushed a little, 'I asked God to help me – I felt He wanted me to find you. I need to get home quickly now because I don't want Mum asking lots of questions. I've written down my phone number. Let me know you are safe, won't you? I do care about you.'

She pushed a piece of paper into his hand and then ran out of the waiting room.

Tiago sat there for a few moments, quite dazed. He didn't know what to do. If Jack was around, and on the warpath, then he might search every station in London to find him. Tiago couldn't believe that accusations of abuse had been levelled at him! The fact that Jack had blamed him probably meant that Tom and Val had told the authorities as he had asked, and Lizzie was now in a safe place. At least that part of his plan had worked.

All the emotional pain rose up in him again. Would he never escape from it? Once more the words came into his mind: 'Run, run, as fast as you can!'

Quickly, he put on his backpack and made for the underground. He would go to the end of the line – as far as he could run – then give himself time to think.

The rush hour was beginning and that was a good thing. He chose the District line and went down to the crowded platform. It was good to get lost in the crowd. Jumping on the first train going east, he found a seat in a corner and travelled all the way to Upminster. Gradually people got off and the train was almost empty by the time it reached its destination. He left the train and went through the barrier – what a blessing his Oyster card had become! Once outside the station, Tiago looked around and decided the best way would be to turn left and walk down the main street, which was lined with shops. It was now dark, and the pavements, though cleared of snow, were icy, so he needed to walk carefully. The last thing he wanted to do was to end up in some hospital with a broken limb!

He had walked about halfway down the road when he came to a main intersection. Seeing a supermarket, he crossed the road and went to buy some food. The next thing was to find a safe shelter for the night.

Not far away was a park, but Tiago couldn't really find a good shelter, so he walked into a residential road. He saw a bungalow which looked very dark and uncared for. The garden was also very overgrown, but there was a shed with the door swinging open. Even though he knew he would leave a lot of footprints, he still decided the shed might be a safe place and not as exposed as sleeping in the park. Inside was dark and Tiago found his torch and had a quick look around. 'No one has been in here for yonks,' he thought to himself, and as he sat on an old chair, the dust rose, causing him to sneeze. He ate his food, then got out his sleeping bag and blanket. He tried to sleep, but his thoughts just wouldn't let him settle. Finally, he decided he must do something to burn away his pain. It was the first time he had self-harmed for days. The pain of the burn did its work – it dulled the pain inside of him and then he managed to sleep.

In the morning, Tiago woke up stiff and cold. It took him a little while to remember where he was and what had happened. Already it was getting light, so he knew he must be on his way again. He tidied up the shed as best he could so that no one would notice that he had eaten and slept there, then peered out of the door. There was still no sign of life in the bungalow, so he took a risk and walked through the garden and out into the street. He saw no one and hoped that no one had seen him.

Once back on the main road, Tiago noticed a café was open. He was glad – he desperately needed a hot drink and a visit to the loo. A couple of guys were having a 'full English' breakfast, and so he took a corner seat and ordered the same, because the smell of the bacon was so wonderful, and made his mouth water.

It was amazing to have something hot to eat and to feel full. Afterwards Tiago made a visit to the loo, had a bit of a wash and tidy-up, and felt ready to carry out the next bit of his plan. He would travel back into central London – in his mind he thought a station like Embankment would be a suitable place – then he would get off and jump in front of the next train that came along. It should be easy to do that on a busy station. He had to get it right – no half measures would do. He couldn't keep running for the rest of his life; he'd end it all. Oblivion must be better than what his life had become. No one would miss him. He was no one and was no use to anyone. It would be for the best. Once again, having made up his mind, he felt empowered and in control.

chapter seven

The underground train rattled along, station after station, and Tiago became more and more agitated. He got out at Embankment station as planned and let that train go on its way. He walked slowly to the very end of the platform, near the tunnel, waiting for the next train to emerge. He was scared stiff, his legs felt like jelly, but his mind could see no other way forward. He moved nearer the platform's edge and heard the faint rumble as the next train approached. His mouth went dry with fear as he made himself ready to jump.

Then he felt a hand on his shoulder pulling him back. Tiago turned to see who was there, and he saw a very large black guy smiling at him.

'You were a bit too near the edge, young man! I was afraid you might topple over and it would be curtains for you – you'd best come back a bit,' he said.

Still shaking, Tiago nodded. The train had come through the tunnel and stopped. The guy looked carefully at the lad and spoke again.

'I'm getting on this one, are you?' he asked.

Once again Tiago nodded, hardly able to speak, and he got in beside the guy. 'I'm just going to Waterloo,' he managed to whisper.

'Stay safe, young man, and remember God loves you.' The guy turned once again to Tiago and gave him an amazing smile. It seemed to warm him inside and help him stop shaking. He got off the train and turned back to wave to the guy, but he couldn't see him in the carriage. He seemed to have disappeared into thin air.

Tiago slowly walked up the stairs to the mainline station. He went to a café and bought himself a cup of hot chocolate. That was a rare treat for he spent his money very carefully, using it only for essentials. Now he needed to stop and think. He thought that perhaps God was real, remembering the sense of peace he had felt in the church, then wondering if God had sent the guy to stop him from committing suicide. As he drank his chocolate slowly, Tiago knew that he couldn't try to throw himself in front of a train again; there must be another way to escape.

The café was at a level above the station forecourt, and Tiago sat and watched people rushing to catch trains. He looked around to see if he could spot any other young people who might be rough sleepers, and to check how many police were about. The weather was still cold, and he would have to find a safe place where he could sleep that night. Then, as he was watching, he noticed a man walking around the station who was obviously looking for someone – and to his utter horror, he saw it was Jack!

Tiago once again began to shake. He pulled his hoodie up so that it covered as much of his face as possible and turned his head away. He gulped down the remains of his drink and walked through the café to the loos. Fortunately, there was a cubicle free, and he went inside and tried to think of what he should do. Would this nightmare never end?

The old rhyme started to come into his mind again: 'Run, run, as fast as you can!' He left the loo and the café and looked over the station once more to see if he could see Jack. He took a very good look, but the man seemed to be gone, so he went down the steps and mingled with the throng of passengers. A train had just come in and a lady came through the barrier using her ticket, but then it dropped from her hand. Tiago picked it up.

'You dropped your ticket,' he said, handing it to her.

She laughed and said to him, 'Did I? I don't need it any more – it's no use to anyone unless they want a one-way ticket to Weymouth today. It's the other half of my day return. Put it in the bin, lad. Thanks,' and she rushed on her way.

Tiago had the ticket in his hand when the announcement was made that the train on platform three was soon to depart to Weymouth. Without a second thought he rushed onto the platform and jumped into the train. As he did, the guard blew his whistle and the train started to ease out of the platform.

There were no seats free, so Tiago began to walk through the train. There were lots of carriages and he slowly made his way to the front because he heard an announcement that the three front coaches were going to Weymouth. He sat down in the corridor and wondered where Weymouth was. He had no idea. He didn't remember ever hearing of such a place – he just hoped that it was miles away from London.

Once the train had travelled for an hour and a half and stopped at Southampton, so many passengers left that there were plenty of seats. The guard had checked his ticket and when the trolley service came around he bought a sandwich and a cola; he was very hungry. The train seemed to get slower and slower as it wound through the smaller towns and villages of Dorset, stopping at every station. Not very many passengers were left when the train eventually pulled into Weymouth and the intercom announced that the train 'terminates here, please will all passengers alight'.

Feeling half-asleep, Tiago put on his backpack and walked down the platform and into the station. He was surprised because it was so small, and the waiting room no more than a few benches in an open area. It didn't look a good place to sleep.

As he walked outside, a blast of cold air hit him. It was just after six o'clock but there were already several rough sleepers in the station forecourt, sitting on the steps with their dogs, and all much older than him. A couple of them were arguing and a police car was waiting at the taxi rank, so Tiago decided that he had better move away from the station area. He had no idea where to go, but having looked up and down the street outside the station, he decided to turn left. He walked up a slight slope to the end of the street, where it joined a main road, the other side of which was a magnificent clock tower and beyond which was the sea. Tiago had only been to the seaside a couple of times in his life – and that was to Brighton. He crossed the road and reached the Esplanade, leant against the railings and gazed out to sea. Laser lights were throwing different colours over the water and it looked beautiful. There were a few ships on the horizon and what he thought was an island. It was all so different from London! However, Tiago knew he had to find a safe place to sleep. A bitterly cold wind was blowing, so curling up on the beach was not an option; the underpass through which had walked seemed too near the town, so he walked along the Esplanade and discovered a park where there were benches. He found one in a sheltered corner, pulled out his sleeping bag and settled down for the night. What a day it had been! Thinking about it, it occurred to Tiago that perhaps, as the guy had told him, God did love him and had given him the train ticket to get to this town.

Even though it was so cold, Tiago slept quite well. He woke when the sky became light, feeling very stiff. In the light of the morning he was able to see the sweep of the bay, the long stretch of sand at one end and pebbles at the other. The tide was in and the sound of the waves was soothing, the salty smell in the air refreshing. It made him feel glad to still be alive, grateful that the big black guy had stopped him from topping himself. Tiago glanced at his watch and saw the date – and realised that it was his birthday! He was fifteen and this was a new beginning!

Tiago walked around the park and found some public loos where he could clean up. Then he decided to find some shops and get some food.

Tiago walked miles that day! He needed to find his way around, look for places where he could sleep at night, cheap places to eat and things he could do through the days. The town looked bright and cheerful, with many places decorated for Christmas. He discovered not one but two shops selling everything for £1 – so stocked up on a few essentials.

The harbour was very interesting and in the inner part there were many, many boats tied up for the winter. The smell of the sea attracted him, and he thought of his father working as a fisherman and his terrible death. One side of the town bridge seemed to have the fishing boats moored, while the other side was more like a marina with boats that were sleek and shiny. Briefly Tiago considered whether he could break into one and use it as a home, but quickly dismissed the thought, not wanting to get on the wrong side of the law and into contact with the police.

Towards the end of that first day, while walking inland, he discovered a yard which looked as if it had once been used to sell sheds, or something like that. It was now deserted, but in the far corner was a long wooden cabin which may have been an office. The door wasn't locked – it looked as if it had once been padlocked but that had been broken long ago. On the outside was a printed notice, now torn and almost illegible, giving a redirection address for post, and the like. Inside, it was an ideal hideaway. There was even a table and a rickety chair – a kitchen area with a sink, and a loo. The lights didn't work, but Tiago presumed the electricity had been cut off. He tried the tap, and much to his surprise, some mucky-looking water came out. He flushed the loo, and heard it refilling, so knew the water was still connected, which was amazing.

Around the yard was a reasonably high fence and an overgrown border with shrubs. On each side of the yard there were chalet bungalows, which had windows in the roofs, but the cabin was quite well hidden from them. Tiago stared at one of them; it seemed so bizarre. The walls were painted bright purple and all the doors a fluorescent green! He was surprised to see that the back garden contained several ancient military vehicles – all looking completely neglected, as was the garden, which was surrounded by a high hedge. The bungalow on the other side was quite different: small and neat, with a drive for cars (but none were there) and pots with shrubs in them.

Not far from this cabin was a small parade of shops – one of which was a mini-market where he could buy food, and another a fish and chip shop. It would be wonderful to have a bag of chips now and then! Outside the shops was a small area of grass and a phone box. An idea came to Tiago. Maybe, if it wasn't vandalised, as the boxes in London so often were, he could phone Tom and just find out if Lizzie was OK. He decided to wait until he found a place to buy a phone card. He had some fears about talking to anyone from his 'old' life, although deep inside he was sure that he could trust Tom and Val, and now, since she'd tried to help him, Zoe-Ann. It was so lonely not having anyone to talk to and he missed Luka, Summer and the rest of the Railway Sleepers' Gang. It had been such a good feeling to belong somewhere.

Within a few days, Tiago had settled into a sort of routine. The days were still very lonely, but since it was so near Christmas, the town looked cheery and the shops were busy. There was a banner on the green near his cabin with a notice announcing that carols would be sung one evening around the Christmas tree outside the shops, so

Tiago went to join in. It was so cool! The lights were twinkling and lots of local people came to sing the carols. He was handed a sheet with the words and joining in the singing made him feel good. It got even better when free hot mince pies and mugs of tea or hot chocolate were passed round. The smell of the mince pies made his stomach rumble and they tasted delicious. For the first time since leaving London, he began to relax. Maybe life here would be good!

chapter eight

The days leading up to Christmas were almost magical for Tiago. Although he still felt lonely, the days were cold and bright, and he found there were lots of people around the town and many special events to celebrate Christmas. Invariably these would be accompanied by food such as mince pies, sausage rolls and chocolate biscuits, along with hot drinks. In all his fifteen years, he had never enjoyed so many treats! He loved singing the carols and hearing the story of the birth of Jesus – if he was honest, he knew nothing about Jesus apart from hearing His name used as a swear word.

The church, in the main street of the town, he discovered was open almost every day of the week, and there was one little corner where, without really being seen, you could go and pray, and also write your concerns down so that other people could pray about them. That corner became a place he sometimes visited, asking God that Lizzie and his mum would be safe, and that he wouldn't be found. He didn't dare write anything down, but he did take a bookmark from a jar there, which said the same thing the guy had told him at Embankment station – that God loved him.

Tiago was glad that there was some water in the cabin where he had taken up residence, but he longed to get properly clean. He wondered if he dared swim in the sea! One evening he counted his remaining money – because he'd been as careful as he could not to waste even one penny, he still had a considerable amount, as Tom had given him so much. He wanted to buy some swimming trunks, so went around all the charity shops in the town to see if he could find any that would fit him. None of them had swimwear on display at Christmas.

There was one shop a bit out of the main town, a charity shop with a café. Here, he could get cheap snacks and drinks, and the clothes were very, very cheap. The staff were kind and chatted to him. They explained that the charity was called Hope House; set up to support and help homeless people. 'There's a house called Hope House near the railway station, where hot meals are served at a very reasonable price, not just to homeless people, but also to the public,' he was told. 'Just look for a small terraced house with a big lantern above the door.'

Tiago bought several items of warm clothing, some swimming trunks and a large towel at this shop, for just a few pounds. His backpack was full as he left and walked into the town centre to find the house he had been told about. It was easy to find as the lantern identified it.

He walked up and down the street but finally decided it might be too risky to go in. If the staff started to ask him questions, he could be discovered as an underage runaway. As well as this, he saw several older guys hanging around the area and he knew from his time as one of the Railway Sleepers' Gang they were often drug users, dealers, or both; maybe even pimps just looking for young lads to influence. He didn't want to go there. There was also a police car parked outside the station and that made him nervous, so, with his heart thumping, he quickly ran back up to the beach and walked back to the main street. Passing a toy shop, Tiago remembered the boy he had seen in Regent's Park on the day he had run away, who was using a skateboard.

'Why didn't I think about it before?' he thought, getting quite excited. 'That's the answer! It would be so cool to use on the Esplanade and a much quicker way to get back to the cabin.' He went into the toy shop and began looking around. 'Lizzie would love these toys,' he thought, touching some of the lovely items on display.

'Can I help you, young man?' an assistant enquired, looking at Tiago quite suspiciously. 'Please pull your hood down – they are not allowed in here.'

'Sorry,' Tiago answered. 'I forgot. It's so cold outside. I came in to look for a skateboard, not too expensive, please.'

The assistant's attitude changed, and he smiled. Tiago thought that perhaps it made a nice change to have a kid who wasn't rude or wanted to shoplift!

He led Tiago to a section of the shop where they had skateboards of various sizes and prices.

'Is it for someone your age or younger?' asked the assistant.

'My age, actually for me,' answered Tiago. 'I've just had a birthday and have some money. I want a strong one, but not too expensive. I thought it would be a good way to get along the Esplanade!'

The assistant helped him choose a suitable skateboard. Then, as he was putting it in a bag and taking the money, he asked, 'Are you good at skateboarding?'

Tiago shook his head.

'Why don't you go to the skatepark, just past the Sea Life Centre, and have a session there before you start on the Esplanade? There's also a free skatepark on Chesil Beach as you go into Portland, and another by the market in Dorchester.'

Leaving the shop, Tiago walked away from the town and along the Esplanade towards the cabin, which he now thought of as 'home'. He saw the skatepark, but it was an indoor centre and certainly not free, so he decided to teach himself. As there were very few people walking along, he took his skateboard out and had a go. He had used one once or twice in the playground when he was at primary school, and the skill soon returned.

It was fun! Even though he was skating into the bitter east wind, he felt good! His cheeks were tingling, and the mile-long stretch to the end of the Esplanade seemed like a quarter of its length on the skateboard. Tiago was delighted with his purchase. He felt as if he really had received a birthday present and could do things that normal boys of his age did.

On the way home, he stopped at the paper shop on the green near the cabin and bought a scotch egg, an apple and some fresh milk. That would make a good meal for the day.

'Hi, Tim,' said the lady in the shop – he went in most days. 'How are things with you?'

'Good, we're all good,' he answered.

'Looking forward to Christmas?' she asked him, in a friendly way.

'Sort of,' he answered. 'We never celebrate much at home – my mum's been sick for years and I don't have a dad.'

'Oh, Tim, I'm sorry to hear that. It's Christmas Eve tomorrow. If you come in for your milk about half past three, I'll be shutting up for the holidays, and if you think your mum would like any of the fresh food, I'll make up a bag for you. I hate to throw it away. I'd rather give it to someone who needs it – if you wouldn't be offended, that is,' she added quickly.

'Oh, that is so cool, thanks,' Tiago answered. 'I'll come around then.'

Tiago found himself humming a Christmas carol as he crossed the road and went through the yard to the cabin. It had been a good day. It wasn't yet dark, and Tiago was getting so used to his new life that he was letting down his guard and didn't notice the net curtain quiver in an upstairs window of the bright purple chalet bungalow nearby, as he opened the cabin door and went inside. These days he left his sleeping bag and blanket at home when he went out for the day. He felt so much more secure that he was getting a bit careless.

It was very cold in the room and Tiago was going to get into his sleeping bag when he heard a faint 'miaow'. There, curled up on his blanket, was the cutest little ginger kitten he had ever seen! The kitten must have come in through the window which was jammed open; he couldn't close it properly.

'Where have you come from?' he asked it. 'Are you lost, or have you run away, too?'

The cat licked his hand, and it made him laugh. Tiago got his milk and poured a drink into a plastic container which had once held a sticky bun. The cat soon emptied it and then curled itself up on Tiago's lap and purred.

'You're a Christmas present to me,' he whispered to it. 'I shall call you Sandy.'

After he had eaten his meal, he crept inside his sleeping bag, pulled up the blanket and, with the kitten curled up on top of it, they both fell asleep.

chapter nine

It was such a surprise on Christmas Eve to wake up and find snow! Everyone had said that Weymouth rarely had snow – but it looked as if it would be a white Christmas this year.

Looking out at the snow brought a slight dilemma. It was so beautiful, but if Tiago left the cabin and walked through the yard, he would leave footprints and that might look very suspicious to any passer-by.

He stroked the kitten, who purred loudly. He knew he had to let him out, so he opened the door a little. Paw prints wouldn't be a problem – but he hoped desperately that Sandy would come back again. In a few minutes the kitten poked his head around the crack in the door and padded in, carrying with him a dead mouse and dropping it at Tiago's feet as a gift! It made Tiago laugh, and he picked up the dead mouse, chucked it out of the door and into the snow.

There was quite a large space inside the cabin, so Tiago practised on his skateboard for a while, until he heard noises outside. Alarm bells rang immediately in his mind and he began to feel panicky. He took a quick peek out of the window, not wanting to give his presence away, but he needed to know what was going on. Outside were two boys and three girls, all younger than him, who had come into the yard and were playing in the snow.

'This is cool,' said one of them. 'It's been empty for months and a great place to play snowballs!'

After a while, the girls started to build a snowman, and the boys joined them. With five of them working, it didn't take long to do it. And they found twigs for arms and small stones for eyes and nose.

They were just finishing when an old lady came out of the purple bungalow next door and shouted at them.

'It's the old woman!' one of the boys said. 'Don't worry about her – she's crazy.'

'I think we should go home, anyway,' the tallest of the girls told them. 'Mum promised hot chocolate at half-past ten and it's later than that.'

The kids waved to the old lady, who was shouting at them, and then disappeared. Tiago was glad. They had messed up the snow so much that no one would notice his footprints and he could go out. This time he was careful to tidy up the cabin and put his sleeping bag, blanket and spare clothes in a cupboard, and remove all evidence of his occupation. If those or other kids came around, he didn't want them to know that someone was living there. He waited a little while to make sure that 'the old woman' had gone back into her bright purple bungalow, then got ready to go out. He intended to leave Sandy in the cabin, but the kitten was determined to follow him. So he picked him up and hid him in the warmth of his anorak. He hid his skateboard – hoping it would be safe – and crept around the bushes and out through the gateway into the road.

It wasn't so easy walking through the snow, but Tiago decided to walk into the town anyway – it was warmer in the shops and he could buy some chips and a drink at the burger bar for his meal. That was OK until Sandy became restless. Tiago knew he had to find a quiet place where he could let the kitten run about for a while. By now he knew his way around the town quite well, so he went to an amusement park and gardens where he could sit down and let the kitten loose. He noticed most of the shops started closing early in the afternoon and it reminded Tiago that he needed to get back to the little shop before half past three, or he would be without milk or food for Christmas. As soon as he stood up to leave, Sandy was at his feet, purring loudly. A rather wet, cold kitten was put back into his anorak, and the pair started to walk home.

Tiago arrived at the shop in the nick of time, and as he reached into the inside pocket of his anorak to get his money, out popped Sandy.

'Goodness, you gave me a fright,' the shopkeeper remarked. 'Don't run around my shop, cat, it's not hygienic! You shouldn't bring a cat in here, Tim.'

'I'm sorry – you see, he's my Christmas present,' explained Tiago. 'He just arrived at the house and started to follow me everywhere, so when I went out this morning, I just put him in my jacket. I didn't want to leave him behind.'

'I see,' the lady said. 'I guess this once it's OK, but please don't bring him again or I might be reported to the public health authority. Anyway, Tim, I've a big bag of food for you – I guess now I should add something for the cat, too.' She went to the deli counter and took out a large slab of pâté and cut off a piece for Sandy, and then added a couple of tins of cat food.

'A happy Christmas to you, Tim,' she said cheerfully. 'I'll be open on Boxing Day for a couple of hours in the morning, if you need anything. Take care of yourself and I hope your mum gets better.'

'Thanks so much,' Tiago answered. 'You're so kind. I hope you have a happy Christmas, too.'

He picked up the large, heavy bag of food, and trudged over the green to the phone box. The thought of spending Christmas Day on his own was making him feel a bit miserable; he wondered so much how Lizzie might be.

Inside his pocket he found the two slips of paper he'd kept so carefully: the telephone numbers of his only friends in the world. For a few minutes he wondered if he dared to phone them – could they trace his whereabouts from a phone box? Could he trust them? He decided he'd take the risk.

First Tiago phoned Tom's number and waited while it rang. Then, when Tom answered, he almost forgot he had to read numbers off the phone card he had bought from the post office.

'Tom,' he said, 'it's me, Tiago. I wanted to call and tell you that I'm OK – but please promise me that you won't grass on me and say I've rung.'

'Oh, Tiago, it's so good to 'ear you. The missus and I 'ave worried so much – are you really OK?' Tom asked.

'Yes,' Tiago answered, 'but what about Lizzie? Is she somewhere safe?'

'Yes, she is, and she'll have the best Christmas of 'er life. She was taken by the social people, put into a 'ome. Then we asked if we could foster 'er, and because they're so short of foster parents, the social worker has been coming three times a week and teaching us the course, and Lizzie 'as just this week come to live with us. We love 'er so much! Val's not 'ere with me – she stays with Lizzie at 'ome. By the way, yer mum is in 'ospital, but the social and police are on 'er case because of drugs found at yer 'ome. That man, 'er boyfriend, accused you of 'urting Lizzie – but we told police what 'appened and they took DNA tests and it proved 'e's the guilty one. 'E's in detention now, waiting for 'is trial. I 'opes 'e gets put down for years – good riddance!'

'Oh, thanks for that news and thank Val for caring for Lizzie. Tell Lizzie I love her and I'll never forget her. I'm so happy Jack's out of the way, but sorry to hear about Mum. I hope she'll get help in the hospital. Have a happy Christmas. Please don't try to find me – when I'm sixteen I'll come and see you. I must go now – my card's running out. Bye.'

Tiago left the phone box, his mind in a spin. He was sad, happy, relieved, scared of being betrayed; all kinds of emotions were whirling around inside him. He didn't notice the kind lady shopkeeper watching him as he left the green and crossed the road. She saw him creep into the old yard where there once had been a fencing and shed works. Something was not right, she knew that. That's why she had packed up all sorts of good food in the bag. He was such a nice lad, but with a distinct London accent – definitely not local. She'd noticed his wrists had scars on them, and there were other marks which looked like burns. She had seen on the TV about young people harming themselves because they had so much pain inside. Was Tim doing this? She decided she would have to ask him a few questions after Christmas, but for now she had to lock up the shop and get home, ready for her family celebrations.

Tiago opened the door cautiously and was relieved to find the cabin just as he had left it. It was brighter than usual; the snow seemed to reflect and make it lighter, but it was bitterly cold, and the wind whistled under the door and through the cracks in the windows. At least he was inside and had food to eat. With excitement, he unpacked the bag – and was amazed at all the things inside. There were oranges, apples, cheese, cakes, bread, sandwiches, ham, pâté, the cat food, baked beans, crisps, cola, even candles, matches, a tin opener, pretty paper plates and serviettes! So many things! There was even a Christmas card – and he put it on the table. He did wonder if the lady had guessed his secret; why else would she include candles? They were red and Christmassy, like he'd seen in the shops, and they would burn for ages.

Sandy was miaowing, so Tiago decided to feed him first before he ate. He looked at the food and thought of the best ways to make it last for a long time. If only Lizzie was here to share it all! Still, it was so cool to know that Tom and Val were caring for her.

That evening, with the candle glowing, his stomach full, feeling cosy in his sleeping bag and the kitten on top of him, Tiago was able to read a book he had bought for just 10p in the charity shop. It was about the Second World War and fighter pilots. For a while he felt happy and free from worries.

That night he slept well, not realising that someone was snooping around the cabin, very quietly, by the light of the moon; and it wasn't Santa Claus!

chapter ten

Tiago woke up on Christmas morning with very mixed emotions. Part of him was happy: he was in a dry place, not out in the open; he felt reasonably safe now that he knew Jack was in custody and couldn't reach him, and he had been cleared of the accusation of abusing Lizzie. That was a huge relief. He also had plenty of food, much more than he would have had at home at Christmas time. There was Sandy, too – a pet for him to love and care for and talk to, even though the only answer was a purr. The other part of him was sad. He wished he had real company; it had been good for the few days when he had been part of a gang, especially when they thought he was some sort of hero. He missed his little sister – he had done so much for her; he missed his jobs at the paper shop and the market; he missed Tom and Val, who had been kind to him; he even missed school – not the bullies, but learning new things, and Zoe-Ann's smile. However, he had had to make a choice, and having run away, there was no going back. Things would be good if only he didn't feel so alone.

After letting Sandy out, Tiago ate a good breakfast. Snow was still hanging around, but now it was slushy. He wondered how to spend the day; all the shops would be shut. He supposed that the churches would be open and maybe the nice church in the centre of the town would have more carols. Did you have to look smart to go to church? Tiago had no idea. He washed his face and combed his hair. He had to admit, the sea air must have done him good because most of his zits had disappeared. He had grown taller in just a few weeks, and even had a few hairs growing on his upper lip and chest. He was growing up and maybe he would soon look more like sixteen than just-turned fifteen.

He chose to wear his thickest sweater – one he had bought from the Hope House shop. He had bought a new beanie hat, too, at the same time. When he felt he looked as smart as possible, he tidied up the cabin, putting everything he could into the cupboard and old filing cabinet. He didn't want Sandy eating all the food, or a stray mouse or rat finding it!

The streets were deserted as he left his adopted home and started the walk into the town. He managed to leave Sandy inside the cabin; he wasn't sure if cats were allowed inside a church. As he arrived at the church and went inside, a lady shook his hand and welcomed him. He crept into one of the back seats, where he hoped nobody would notice him. It was warm, and he took off his anorak and hat, feeling quite smart in his sweater.

There were carols to sing, and then a short talk about the birth of Jesus. After the service was over, people went into a room at the side of the church where hot drinks and mince pies were served. A guy stood up and gave out a notice to everyone present that he was cooking Christmas dinner; about twenty people were coming, and anyone else in the congregation was welcome to stay.

'Are you on your own, son?' a lady asked him. 'If you would like to stay, there is no charge and it will be fun.'

'Really, may I?' Tiago answered. 'Thanks, that's cool.'

The Christmas dinner was amazing. Tiago helped by getting tables set up, and it made him happy to be useful and have people to chat to. Everyone staying for the meal seemed to be friendly and, best of all, no one asked him any awkward questions. At the meal there were crackers with jokes and hats as well as wonderful food: roast turkey with all the trimmings, followed by Christmas pudding and trifle. The smell of it was great, let alone the taste. Tiago cleared his plate completely. He didn't remember ever feeling so full up before.

After the meal he helped clear up the dishes. With lots of people helping, it didn't take long. Then tables were pushed back to the walls, and the chairs put into a semicircle in front of a large screen. The person who was organising the meal used his laptop to project a movie, an old Disney film called *Fantasia*, which Tiago had not seen before. Most of the older people seemed to know the music which was being played as Mickey Mouse got up to all sorts of antics. It was just silly and funny, and everyone was laughing, including Tiago. He thought that this was what it must be like to be in a real family – something he had never known. Afterwards they all played some party games, which were fun, though Tiago couldn't help thinking that people at his old school in Islington would probably think it was all very boring; not at all a cool way to spend Christmas afternoon.

After the games, he was sure it must be time for everyone to go home, but a lady put the kettle on and announced that tea would be ready in a little while. Once again, the tables were set up and loaded with sausage rolls, sandwiches, cheese straws, crisps and cakes. It was wonderful! Tiago was still too full to eat very much, but he did enjoy it. Suddenly, there was a loud knock at the door and everyone shouted, 'Come in!' Someone dressed as Santa Claus walked in, carrying a large sack. Each person in the room was given a gift – and there were, in fact, thirty-two people present. Tiago was amazed at such kindness.

When he was given his gift, the 'Santa' spoke to him and told him that God loved him. Today, although he still didn't understand it, he found that he could believe it. These people had made him feel special and wanted, and he had been happy.

When it was time to go home and he was putting on his anorak and hat, the guy who had cooked the meal came over.

'Did you enjoy yourself, Tim?' he asked him.

'Oh, yes, thank you so much. It's been so cool; the best Christmas I've ever had.'

'We're so pleased you could join us. You will always be welcome here. If we can ever help you in any way, just get in contact,' he was told, and the guy handed him a card with phone numbers on it. 'I also work in the week at Hope House if you need a meal, shower or any help. The house is by the station.'

'I've seen it,' answered Tiago, 'but I've never been inside. Maybe I will stop by sometime.'

Tim walked back to the cabin in the dark. The sky was clear, and he could see lots of stars, as well as a bright moon. It was rare to see stars in the London night sky; somewhere in the back of his mind he remembered it was because of light pollution or some such thing. The cold east wind had died down and the snow had almost disappeared. There were bright lights in the houses and gardens and everything looked cheerful. He felt cheerful, too, even singing carols to himself as he walked along the roads.

When he let himself into the cabin, Sandy came rushing over and rubbed himself around Tiago's legs.

'Good to see you, too, mate,' he said, picking up the kitten and giving him a cuddle. 'Guess you're hungry. I'll light a candle and fix you some food.'

When the candle was lit, Tiago looked around the cabin and had a strange sense that things had been moved or someone had visited. He couldn't put his finger on what it was that was different – maybe a strange smell? However, it made him uneasy and took away his happiness. He had almost forgotten that he was a runaway and that the police might still be looking for him.

The present Tiago had been given was a book, and he was thrilled with it. It was the story of a young man in the army who had gone to Afghanistan, and he couldn't wait to read it. There was also a small booklet, called *John*. Both were put inside his backpack. They might make it even heavier, but they were treasures and reminders of a 'proper' Christmas Day.

As soon as Sandy had finished eating, Tiago blew out the candle and snuggled down into his sleeping bag, with a contented kitten on top of him.

Waking the next morning, the sense of unease grew greater, even though he didn't know why. He opened the door to let Sandy out into the yard and was terrified to see an elderly lady, dressed in old military clothes, pointing a shotgun at him. It seemed like a horror movie or a dream; he couldn't believe what he was seeing, nor could he find his voice. He felt his mouth go dry and his legs began to shake. Total fear took hold of him.

'You thought I didn't know you were here?' she croaked at him. 'I've been watching you every day since you came. I'm good at surveillance – trained to do it, you see. Nothing gets past my eyes. You have no right here. You are an enemy of the nation!'

She pushed the shotgun almost into his chest, and Sandy wailed, his back up and his hair standing on end.

'Get inside,' the woman commanded, pushing Tiago back into the cabin with the barrel of the shotgun. Once inside, she closed the door and put her back against it, never for a moment taking her eyes off him.

'Who do you think you are, breaking into this cabin, and who are you spying for?' she said, roughly.

Tiago had realised that she must be the old woman from the purple bungalow – the one where ancient military Land Rovers stood around the garden like sculptures. No wonder the kids making the snowman there had called her 'crazy'! If she really was then she might be completely unpredictable. Tiago was shaking visibly, and felt so sick that he thought he was going to throw up. His heart was pounding so loudly he was sure she would hear it. In his head, he prayed, 'God, if You *do* love me, help me!'

'What have you got to say for yourself? You had better confess before I blow your head off!' she shouted.

Where the words came from, Tiago didn't know, but suddenly he felt calm and more in control.

'Missus,' he said, his voice at last coming back to him, 'I'm no spy, just a runaway kid looking after a stray cat. If you shoot me, you'll end up in prison for the rest of your life. If you do shoot me, you'll be doing me a favour. I tried to jump in front of a train before Christmas, but a man saved me, so I came here – but I wanted my life to end. So, go ahead, shoot!'

Tiago couldn't believe he'd said that – it just came out of his mouth.

For a few seconds the woman looked undecided, and Sandy jumped at her, little kitten though he was, making her drop the gun. In a flash, Tiago grabbed it, but he hadn't the courage to point it at the crazy old woman.

Suddenly, she seemed to crumble, her bravado all gone. She just looked like a pathetic old lady. The skin on her face and hands was wrinkled and she had a large hump on her back. Tiago didn't feel scared of her any more – she looked so old and sad.

'You shouldn't be living here, you're a trespasser,' she mumbled.

'Come to that, you are trespassing, too,' replied Tiago. 'I don't want you to get into trouble, you'd best go back to your bright purple bungalow and make yourself a cup of tea.'

'My purple bungalow – that's for my daughter. She always loved bright purple. I had it painted for her. One day she will come back home. She ran away many years ago.' A big tear trickled down the old lady's cheek, and Tiago felt sorry for her.

'It's Christmas,' he said. 'Would you like a mince pie to have with your tea? I've got some nice ones. Would you like a sausage roll, too? I didn't steal them – the lady in the shop gave them to me on Christmas Eve.'

The old lady looked at Tiago and gave him a bit of a smile so, still holding the shotgun, he wrapped up a little package for her. He gave it to her and she mumbled, 'Thanks,' and went away. Tiago let out a huge sigh of relief. He picked up Sandy and cuddled him. 'That was so scary,' he whispered. 'You were so amazing, saving me. Thank you.'

chapter eleven

Tiago sat on the chair and Sandy jumped on his lap. He stroked the kitten and it calmed him a little, for he was still feeling very shaken by the whole event. The old lady was clearly mentally unstable, and she could easily have shot him.

'You are one cool cat,' he told Sandy. 'You saved my life. Are you some kind of angel cat to do that? You're awesome!'

The kitten just purred.

'Now we must think,' he said aloud. 'We can't stay here any longer. I shall have to get back on the road again. That old lady is unstable and probably will go to the police or tell all the neighbours about me. Where shall I go? If I go to the town, the police might catch up with me. I wish I knew what to do.'

Tiago started to pack his belongings very carefully into his backpack. It wasn't easy to get everything in and it was much heavier than before. He and Sandy ate as much food as they could, and he tidied the place up. Then there was the question of the shotgun. What should he do with it?

The last thing Tiago wanted was to carry an offensive weapon around with him. He had no idea if it was loaded or not. If he left it in the cabin, then someone else might get hold of it and misuse it, or the police might think it was his. It would have his fingerprints on it.

After thinking about the situation for a while, Tiago thought of a solution. He would go into the garden next door and put the gun into one of the old Land Rovers – hopefully the old lady wouldn't find it, but it did belong to her, so he was only returning her property.

The ground was still a bit slushy outside, but he managed to creep around the hedge and behind one of the cars, then, seeing the window was open, he pushed the gun inside. He looked at the purple bungalow but saw no movement. With any luck, the old lady would be tucking into her mince pies and sausage roll! Tiago crept back to the cabin, put on his backpack, hid Sandy inside his jacket, and carried his skateboard under his arm.

In his mind, once again, he heard the mantra: 'Run, run, as fast as you can! You can't catch me...'

Would this be his life forever? Would his mother one day be an old, crazy, sad woman waiting for a runaway son to return? Tiago tried to push the thought out of his mind. He was afraid of the future, but also afraid of turning back – to be put into care and to return to school to be bullied again.

The backpack, kitten and skateboard made things considerably more difficult for Tiago as he set off. He knew there was a small road that went through the ridge of hills behind where he had been living, and wound its way to Dorchester, the county town. It was only about six miles to walk. Maybe a new town would provide new opportunities for shelter and security.

Tiago found the road easily. It was just around the corner from the purple bungalow. The old lady's home had high hedges around it, so he could walk past without being seen by her, should she be spying again. The road was deserted, but it was pleasant to walk along, because on each side were large, interesting houses with front gardens. There were lots of trees and on one side ran a small stream. There was no pavement, so Tiago kept close to the edge of the road, walking to face the oncoming traffic. He wished he had some reflective bands on his anorak; being a 'townie' it hadn't occurred to him before how helpful that would be on a country road.

The houses lined the road for about half a mile, then it began to rise, steeply. Behind the houses, on each side, he could see the hillsides, still with a little snow on the top, and on the left-hand side, he noticed cows grazing. Coming from London, he had seen very few cows and he was interested that they seemed to be in a straight line right on the top ridge of the hill.

The houses petered out and Tiago was walking through a gorge, with fields and then hills on each side. In the fields on the left were several horses, looking rather miserable and cold, even though they were wearing coats. As he walked up, the horses came to the fence. He wished he had apples or carrots or something else to give them. Crossing the road with care, Tiago went to stroke their faces. They were huge! He had never been that close to a horse before.

A car drove past him and he jumped a little. He had best get back on the right side of the road! On the other side, it was a rocky hillside, with outcrops of chalk, brambles and bushes.

Walking up the steep hill caused him to stop for breath several times, and he was glad when he could see the summit; at least, he thought it was, but later realised that it was a plateau, with yet another steep hill beyond that. He comforted himself with the thought that eventually it must go downhill again and that would be easier. The bare, rocky hillside gave way to fields where the road plateaued and sheep were happily munching on the grass. It was wet and muddy after the snow, but they didn't seem to mind.

Beyond the fields on the right-hand side were a few buildings. From a distance they looked like old farm outbuildings, but as he got nearer, Tiago could see that the first one was a new construction, not yet completed. Even so, it had a sort of deserted look. Beyond this were old barns and what appeared to be a tumbledown house.

'Good,' he said to Sandy. 'This is somewhere we can rest.' He had probably only walked two miles, he figured, but already he was tired. Sandy was wriggling about inside his anorak, so he guessed the kitten needed to run around.

Coming to the gate of the old farmyard, Tiago realised that, hidden from the road by bushes and brambles, there was a caravan – not an ordinary caravan, but the shape of a gypsy vardo.

He unzipped his coat and Sandy immediately jumped out and ran into the yard. Tiago had to follow because he didn't want to lose his kitten.

'What the dickens are you up to?' a gruff voice asked him, but not unkindly. Tiago looked up and saw a man with a rather long, greying beard coming out of the gypsy caravan.

'My kitten has just run into your yard,' he answered. 'I don't want to lose him!' With that he started to call Sandy.

A woman appeared. 'What's all the commotion?' she enquired.

'Nothing, love,' answered the man. 'This lad's cat has run into the yard – I guess the cat has smelt a rat or something.' He turned to Tiago. 'Where are you going, son, with that heavy load on your back, on Boxing Day?'

'I'm walking to Dorchester,' Tiago answered. 'These hills are very steep, and I think I've only walked a couple of miles – could I rest for a few minutes?'

'No problem, son,' the woman said at once. 'You look like you're a traveller. We're travelling people, too, and we always make fellow travellers welcome.'

Tiago was so glad to take his backpack from his shoulders and put his skateboard down. He sat on the step of the vardo. He not only felt tired but also discouraged at having to move on again.

'Fancy a drink?' the woman asked him. 'By the way, I'm Daisy and my husband is Dan.'

Tiago's defences instantly went up – could he trust this couple? They appeared to be genuine travellers and harmless enough, but you never could be sure. The crazy old woman in the bungalow had frightened him so badly he'd gone on the run again! Yet he felt really tired and very thirsty. A drink sounded lovely, so he decided to take the risk.

'Thanks, I'd love a drink,' Tiago replied. 'My name's Tim – Tim Cox.'

'Well, come inside out of the cold and we'll have a brew,' Dan suggested.

Inside the caravan it was surprisingly spacious, and very neat. It was warm and cosy, and Tiago gladly sat in the chair offered to him.

The couple seemed kind and friendly, and gradually Tiago's reserve began to fall away so that soon the three of them were chatting together.

'We're spending the winter here,' explained Dan, 'then we'll move on when the weather gets better. Most of us who are true Romanies have farms which we visit at certain times of the year.'

'Do you always come here, then?' asked Tiago.

'Yes,' answered Dan. 'When I was just a lad, about your age, I guess, my family began coming to this farm. It was a large working farm in those days, and we helped the farmer with his stock during the winter.'

'What did you do after the winter?'

'When spring came we would move on and join other members of our family in various parts of the country. We helped farmers with fruit and vegetable harvesting, then worked in the hop fields in Kent; followed by the apple and pear harvest in Somerset in September and October.'

'Wow, that sounds like fun, but didn't you have to go to school?' Tiago asked.

'We went to local schools if we stayed in one place for more than a few days – not that I learned very much. I was a poor student and can barely read or write. Nowadays, the travellers' children must attend school properly and get a good education,' Dan told him.

'Is this still a working farm?' asked Tiago, looking around the yard. 'It doesn't seem to have anyone living in the old farmhouse any more. That new house looks abandoned, too.'

'There's a bit of a story about that,' continued Dan. 'The old farmer – I knew him when I was a youngster – died some years ago, and his wife went into a nursing home. She's passed on now, too. Before he died, Farmer Jim, as we called him, sold his farm to another local farmer living in a nearby village, but in the deeds of sale there was a clause to say that the Daniel Smith family of gypsies were to be allowed to continue to winter here. The new farmer wasn't altogether pleased about that, but he had no choice. It was all legal.

'We continued coming every winter, but the new farmer didn't want to live in the old farmhouse; he preferred his own house in the village. Nothing's been done to improve the old house, so it's not in a very good state and some parts of it we don't use.

'Then, must be coming on ten years ago now, the farmer decided to build a new house on the plot of land. He was doing it with his four sons in their spare time, and his plan was to let it out to visitors in the summer. He got on well with the building, as you can see, but then the council found that he had no planning permission and he had to stop work. He was never given the permission, and so it has remained in that state ever since!'

'Such a waste,' said Daisy. 'I don't think it will ever be finished now, even if they got all the papers signed. The farmer's boys are all married and have nice houses for their families – it's not as if they would want it, and it's a bit far out for visitors 'cos there's no shops or buses and it's a couple of miles either way to get to the next village or down to Weymouth.'

'So,' added Dan, 'we still come here, living mostly in our own caravan, but there is water in the taps in the old farmhouse, and a well in the garden, plus a generator for electricity. That means we can heat water, and Daisy uses bottled gas for her cooking – she's never used electric for cooking, and when we travel we use gas. When we want to have a bath, we go into the old farmhouse; the bathroom is still useable, but we're not really "house" people; we love our old vardo. It's so mild here we don't find it cold. It's very rare to have snow like we've just had.

'We can use the old house as much as we want to; most of it is set up and still furnished. The end part over there,' he went on, pointing to the far end of the building, 'the roof isn't good, so we don't use those rooms; otherwise, it's not too bad. We help the farmer by keeping an eye on the sheep in the field – you'd be surprised how many livestock rustlers there are these days.

'See up there, son?' Dan asked, pointing to a glass-fronted locked cupboard under the curved roof of the vardo. 'That's my shotgun – only to be used if any animals try to attack the sheep. I hope I never have to use it, but it's one way I can thank the farmer for honouring our right to stay here.'

Tiago began to shake when he saw the shotgun. Daisy and Dan looked at each other in alarm.

'Tim, what's the matter? Is it the gun? It's only there as a precaution. I would never use it unless it was a dire emergency,' Dan told him.

'I'm sorry,' Tim replied. 'It's just that someone threatened me this morning with a shotgun, and it was only because Sandy, my cat, jumped on the woman and she dropped it that I'm here and still alive. It's why we took to the road again and are walking to Dorchester. I ought to find Sandy and get on my way.'

'Oh, son, how awful!' exclaimed Daisy. 'What a terrible thing to happen to you – and at Christmas, too! You say it was a woman who did this? What sort of woman would do such a thing?'

'I think she was a bit crazy,' answered Tiago. 'She was old, wore army clothes and had been snooping around the place where I was living. She accused me of being a spy. Some of the children who were playing in the yard the day it snowed called her "crazy". She scared me so much, I really think she would have shot at me if Sandy hadn't jumped.'

Dan looked at Tiago with such kindness that he felt like crying.

'Tim, why don't you tell us about yourself? Maybe we can help you,' said Dan. 'I knew the moment you came into the yard that you were in trouble and maybe had run away from home. We won't, I promise you, tell your story to anyone or give you away. We gypsies are none too fond of the police. Over the centuries we've been given a pretty rough time because we're travellers and prefer to move around, as Romanies always have, but we look after each other and help each other out when there are problems. We've had three boys of our own, and sometimes we've had nephews and nieces living with us and a grandkid as well. Trust us, we'll understand.'

Tiago looked at the couple and could see and hear nothing but sincerity and warmth. He was still unsure about trusting them with his story – after all, half an hour ago they were complete strangers. He'd always thought gypsies were not to be trusted, yet he badly needed to ask for advice. He was tired, and scared that he would be running away every few days trying to find new places to live and keep away from druggies and pimps who might take advantage of him; he was frightened that he would never be able to settle down and have a normal life again. Somehow, when he had decided to run away, he hadn't thought about the long term; he just knew he had to get out of his situation and have some control over his life. After a few minutes' thinking, he decided to take the risk.

'Can I really trust you with my story?' he asked. 'Will you really promise not to tell the police or social services about me?'

Daisy put her arm on Tiago's shoulder. 'We'll never tell your story to anyone unless you tell us we can. I know most people think we're not trustworthy, but we have our own code of honour and both of us promise to keep mum about anything you tell us, don't we, Dan?' she said, looking at her husband, who nodded his head in agreement.

'OK,' said Tiago, 'I'll tell you.'

chapter twelve

Tiago began at the beginning, telling the couple some of his story. It took a quite a while, because at times, Tiago got upset and had to stop to control his emotions. Daisy and Dan were visibly moved by what he had to say. They listened attentively, asking a question every now and then.

'I understand why you ran away, Tim. By the way, can we still call you Tim?' asked Dan.

'Please do. I feel comfortable with it now,' he answered.

'Why don't you stay with us and eat lunch? Daisy has a nice stew on the stove. It will give us time to think about how we can help,' Dan said.

Tim agreed, and went to explore the bathroom in the old farmhouse and find his kitten, while they talked over the situation.

As he went through the farmyard, Tiago was feeling good because he'd told the truth to Dan and Daisy. He was fed up with telling lies, and somehow he sensed he could trust them.

With Sandy in his arms, he went back to the cosy vardo. If their caravan was anything to judge by, they were good, clean people. It was such a contrast to the house where he had been brought up, although he had tried to keep it a bit clean and tidy.

'Good, dinner is ready,' Daisy told him, smiling. 'Dan has an idea, and I think it's a good one!'

'Yes,' said Dan. 'We wondered if you would like to stay here with us through the winter. It's the worst time of year for anyone to be on the road. You can sleep in the farmhouse; some of the rooms are OK and there's an electric fire in the bedroom, which you can use when the generator is on. That way, you will have your own space. Daisy will cook for you and do your washing – she's so excited to have another boy to care for – and in return, you can help me with the sheep.

'What do you think about that idea? When the spring arrives, you can decide what you want to do: travel with us or make your own way again. If anyone asks us, we can say you are a grandson – with your dark hair and eyes you would pass easily for a Romany.'

Tiago was quite overwhelmed by the offer. He really didn't have to think long about the proposal. It was so cold, and sleeping rough in Dorchester would be difficult. He had no idea if he'd be safe in that town. Here at least he'd be in a dry house and there would be hot food. He could take to the road again if things didn't work out, so he decided to take the risk.

'Do you really want me to stay around?' he asked. They nodded their heads. 'Then I'd like to. It will be so cool to have Romany friends. Would you mind if I called you Dan and Daisy? I promise not to be any trouble, and when the ground warms up, I could help you with the garden. I love working in gardens.' Tiago was smiling from ear to ear.

'Good. That's settled, then,' said Daisy. 'Let's take your things to the farmhouse and make up a bed for you.'

They walked over to the old building, and Sandy, who had disappeared once again, scuttled out of the barn, followed by a sheepdog, who was barking loudly.

'Be quiet, Shep!' commanded Dan. 'This is Tim, and he is your friend! He's a friendly dog, Tim, and helps round up the sheep, and he doesn't seem to mind your cat.'

'Wow!' exclaimed Tiago when he saw the bedroom. 'It's huge!' There was a wardrobe and a cupboard which locked; a double bed, which Daisy soon made up for him; a bedside light and an old TV set. 'I've never seen a room like it!' he exclaimed. 'I thought this house was tumbling down!'

'The roof is leaking and falling in at each end of the building, but the middle part is still in reasonable condition. Old Farmer Jim and his wife used this room and left everything for us, so it's all legit, so to speak. You've already discovered the bathroom next door and know the plumbing works. We use that, too, but we won't come into your room and disturb you. There's no running hot water, but we heat some up every day,' explained Daisy. 'Now you unpack, get settled and then come back to the vardo and we'll show you round the whole farmyard.'

Tiago unpacked his backpack. He couldn't believe his good fortune. There was something about the couple that made him feel safe, in the way he did with Val and Tom. He put his clothes away and put his two books on the bedside table. When everything was sorted, Tiago took the remaining food he still had with him over to the vardo.

'Daisy,' he said shyly, 'here's the food I had with me. Please take it and use it up. I have some money, too, and that'll help pay for my food.'

'You keep that, Tim, you may need it sometime at a future date. Dan and I have enough to keep us all. Keep it locked in your room or, if you like, we have a small safe in the vardo and we'll look after it until you need it, and any other valuables you might have.'

'I don't have much,' Tim told her, 'just the rest of my wages from working in the market and from my paper round; my birth certificate and a couple of copies of other documents. I'll bring them over.'

It had turned a bit wet and drizzly but, with Shep and Sandy at their heels, Dan set out with Tiago to show him the farmyard. Next to the old house where Tiago had his room was a barn where once the cattle had been housed. Then there was an open barn, just walls and a tin roof covering it. Here Daisy had washing lines and big tubs of water, gas cylinders and a stove where she cooked and heated water. Next to that was another, smaller barn. Inside were sheep pens and a floor covered with straw. A couple of farm cats arched their backs when they saw Sandy – but he took no notice. Shep yapped at them and they took no notice of him, either. It made Tiago laugh.

'They are all good enough friends, really,' said Dan. 'They just don't like to show it in public! These are the sheep pens we use when we need to inspect the sheep. Sometimes the ewes need help with lambing. We'll be using them soon. Some ewes are almost ready to drop. I

91

mean, to give birth to their lambs,' he explained. 'I'll be glad of your help then. Here in the West Country it's so mild that we can lamb from autumn onwards – the only part of the country it happens.'

Then they walked past the new building – it seemed such a shame that it had just been abandoned. Most of the construction was finished, but none of the inside work. The windows weren't glazed, just covered with thick polythene which flapped around in the wind. Behind the new house was a garden, looking dead and neglected, but Tiago guessed that his plot in Islington would be looking drab, too. It was December – not gardening weather.

Behind the garden was a drystone wall, with a gate in it. They walked through the gate and into the field, which was very wet and boggy. Tiago looked in dismay at his trainers, which were his only footwear.

'Don't worry, Tim. I'm sure I can find you some wellies. This field has springs in it and floods as soon as there is any rain. You can see the rushes growing. Daisy has used these for years to weave baskets, and she used to sell them at fairs and the like. It gets drier as we walk up the hill.'

At the top of the hill there were amazing views all the way down to the sea. Sheep were grazing, sheltering in ridges which ran around the hill.

'This is an ancient hill fort,' Dan told him. 'There are lots of historical sites around this part of Dorset. The sheep love the shelter that the ridges give, especially if the wind is blowing off the sea.'

Dan showed Tiago how to inspect the feet of the sheep and make sure they had no 'foot rot'. Tiago was a bit scared of the animals at first, never having been that near to sheep or, for that matter, any farm animals, and they seemed much larger than when he had seen them from the road.

'You'll get used to them, Tim. They aren't such silly creatures as people think,' Dan told him.

Tiago found that to be true as he settled into his new life at the farm over the next few days. He loved it, even though there was a lot of wet and dismal weather that winter. Once or twice Dan needed his help in the night with ewes who were having trouble birthing. It wasn't a big flock, so the farmer was happy to leave Dan in charge. He had another large flock on the other side of his farm, in the fields by the white horse that was carved into the hillside.

One ewe gave birth to triplets. These were small, so the ewe and the lambs were brought into the barn where Tiago helped to hand-rear the smallest one by feeding it milk from a baby's bottle. He loved doing that, and called the lamb 'Snowflake', even though all traces of snow had long gone.

The days passed happily into weeks and Tiago felt really part of the Smith family. Dan and Daisy treated him with kindness and respect, and never questioned him about where he was going or what he was doing when he went out on his own. In fact, he normally only went for long walks in the countryside, usually with Shep at his heels. He didn't need to go to town for shopping because Dan took his old pick-up truck to Dorchester each Wednesday, which was market day. Occasionally, Tiago and Daisy went with him. Dan had found him some wellies and trainers, for he was growing quickly and had outgrown his own shoes. One day, Dan took him to get new jeans as he was getting so tall. It was so good having a father figure to teach him things – including how to shave and to buy him a razor.

In return for all their kindness, Tiago dug the garden and planted broad beans and then other vegetables as the days got longer and the weather became milder. He loved the feel of the soil and thought that he might like to become a gardener as his mother's father had been. He watched all the TV programmes about gardening, learning all he could.

From time to time he still had nightmares about his mum's boyfriend, Jack, coming into his room, and he wondered if the trial had taken place and how long he had been 'sent down' for. There was no phone box near the farm, but one Wednesday Tiago decided to go to the market with Dan. He wanted to visit the post office and buy another phone card to ring Tom and find out any news.

'Hi, Tom,' Tiago said. 'I'm phoning from our local market. It's a bit different from Islington market, although it's pretty crowded! I wanted to find out how you're doing, and how Lizzie is.'

'Great to 'ear yer, Ti,' answered Tom. 'Missus and I've bin wondering 'ow yer doing. Val and Lizzie 'ave just arrived to do the shopping, so yer can talk to 'er. 'Old on a minute.'

'Lizzie, you do remember me, don't you?' asked Tiago. 'I've gone away and am working on a farm. I help feed the baby lambs – it's such fun! I hope you're being a good girl for Aunty Val. One day I'll come back and see you. I love you, Lizzie.'

Lizzie's little voice piped up, 'Love you, too, Ti, and I's being a very good girl!'

Tiago had to wipe a tear from his eye, and then he heard Val's voice telling him about his mother. 'Yer ma was in 'ospital, but then the police got 'er fer selling drugs. She's already had 'er trial and bin sent to prison. I think they 'ope to 'elp 'er there. Yer best off staying where you are. 'Elping at a farm, yer told Lizzie? That's good. Yer always 'ave a 'ome with us, so don't yer forget that. Bye, Ti.'

Then Tom came on the line again and started to tell him that Jack was due to appear in court again very soon and he was sure he'd be sent to prison for a long time, so he didn't have to worry about seeing him ever again.

'By the time 'e's released on parole, you'll be a man. Like Val said, we'll always 'ave a 'ome fer you. Lizzie will live with us long term and if ever it's possible, we'd like to adopt 'er as our daughter. Well, she's like our daughter already.'

After talking to them all, Tiago felt reassured and comforted that he had other people who cared about him, although he started to shake a bit and his legs went to jelly when Tom talked about Jack. He told Tom all about his new friends, Dan and Daisy. Tom promised not to tell anyone where he was and what he was doing. He had, however, asked for an address, because he wanted to send a surprise to Tiago. Rather reluctantly, Tiago had agreed and given the address of the farm and said to send it care of Dan Smith.

'Please, as soon as you have sent it, tear it up and burn the address,' he begged, and Tom promised to do that.

chapter thirteen

A couple of days later, the postman's van stopped at the gate of the farmhouse. He carried a small package, addressed to Dan. Everyone was surprised because the postman had never visited them before! Tiago was so glad he had given his address to Tom, for in the parcel, carefully wrapped, was a photo. The photo was of his sister, Lizzie, looking so cool in nice jeans and a sweater with a fairy on the front. Her hair was brushed and tied back with a red ribbon. She looked so well and happy and his heart almost burst with pride and joy. The photo was in a leather frame. He could put it by his bed and say goodnight to Lizzie every evening when he put out his light. Inside the package, too, was an envelope with some money and a note, very badly written, but Tiago knew that Tom wasn't very good at either writing or reading. The note told him to buy some new clothes because he must have grown a lot living in the country.

Tiago went rushing to Dan and Daisy and showed the lovely photo of his sister, and then gave the money to them.

'You should have this,' he said. 'You've bought food for me and helped me so much.'

'No, that's for you and you deserve it. You've helped us a lot these past few weeks. Anyway, you'll need new clothes for the summer, you're growing so fast! I'll put it away in the safe if you like, until you want to spend it,' Dan answered.

'Thanks so much, Dan,' responded Tiago, giving him and Daisy a hug.

A few more weeks passed by without incident. Spring had arrived, and everywhere was looking green and fresh. Tiago loved it. He continued his long walks with Shep, exploring the beautiful countryside around the farm. Sometimes Dan came with him and taught him the names of the wild flowers, bushes and trees. From time to time they walked down to the sea. It was quite a long way and Tiago always felt a little nervous when he went past the bright purple bungalow with the fluorescent green doors and thought of the crazy old woman and the shotgun. He only ever went that way when Dan was with him, because he felt safer with him. When they went, Tiago liked to take his skateboard, and while Dan sat on a bench looking out to sea, he skated up and down the Esplanade.

They didn't mention it very often, but Tiago knew he needed to soon decide whether to stay in Weymouth, find new pastures further afield, or go with the Smiths when they embarked on their summer trek. He was aware if he did the latter, it would be a hardship for the old couple to share the vardo with someone else; even though they had told him there was a tent he could use, there really wasn't much room or privacy for three people to live, plus the dog and cat.

In the end two things happened that forced him to make up his mind. The first occurred in the early hours one morning. Tiago was woken up by a noise. Shep, who now always slept at his feet, began to growl, and this made him realise something wasn't right. Suddenly, the door to his room burst open and in came two guys, both looking like rough sleepers, because they had backpacks and were unshaven. Tiago could smell alcohol on their breath. Terror rushed through him, his mouth going dry and his body beginning to shake. Shep growled loudly at them and then started to bark. One of the guys went to kick him, but he ran between his feet and out of the room. Tiago hoped that he'd gone to the vardo to wake Dan. Meanwhile, the guys pulled him roughly off the bed. They were bigger than he was and hurt him as they dragged him off.

'We'll have this nice pad. Get your stuff and get out!' They began to throw Tiago's things around and opened the wardrobe and found his backpack. One of them picked up his book about the fighter pilots and threw it at him. It hit him near the corner of his eye and he let out a yell of pain. The guys laughed in a horrid way, bringing back the memories of the bullies at school. Tiago was too scared even to talk, and grabbed his photo of Lizzie, his books and began to stuff them into his bag. The guys were so drunk that he dared not cross them in any way, for he'd learned from bitter experience that when his mother and Jack were drunk they were extremely unpredictable, and it was better just to keep quiet and get out of their way.

'Hurry up – get out of here! This is our pad now. Get yourself on the road!' shouted one.

Then the door opened and Shep sidled up to Tiago. Behind him was Dan, with his loaded shotgun.

'Over in that corner, you two, hands on your heads!' Dan shouted, startling the men, who had been too drunk to notice the door opening. One of them tried to grab Tiago, as if to take him hostage and make him a human shield, but Shep was too fast for him, and went for him, grabbing his trouser leg. His growl was ferocious, and the guy had no way of knowing that he wasn't an aggressive animal. He swore and went to kick Shep, but being drunk, he ended up falling over. Tiago hid behind Dan.

'One more move from either of you and I won't hesitate to shoot!' Dan warned them. 'Tim, Daisy has phoned for the police. Run and get me some rope from the barn and we'll tie these guys up until they come.'

Tiago ran, suddenly getting some strength back into his legs, and glad to escape. Shep and Dan guarded the intruders, but they were bullies and cowards, and all their bravado had disappeared at the sight of the gun. They made no move to try to escape. By the time Tiago had found the rope, Daisy was also heading to the farmhouse – dressed, armed with her meat cleaver, and looking very angry. Tiago could see that she also was a force to be reckoned with! Between them, they tied the guys' hands.

What a relief it was to hear the sound of the police siren coming up the road. Even though he was still scared of the police, Tiago ran out to guide them to where the intruders were.

'Oh, it's you two again, is it?' one of the officers said, obviously recognising the guys, 'and drunk and disorderly, too. Let's get the handcuffs on and untie these ropes.'

It didn't take long before the guys were in the police car and being driven away, but the three of them were so shaken that they couldn't just go back to sleep, so Daisy went to make some tea.

'Come into the vardo for the rest of the night – we'll make a bed on the floor,' suggested Dan. Tiago was relieved; he wasn't looking forward to going back to his room. 'Anyway,' Dan continued, 'the police might want fingerprints in the morning. It's best not to disturb it too much.'

Mention of the police returning and fingerprinting freaked out Tiago. He didn't sleep all night because all sorts of worries came flooding into his mind. The last thing he wanted was the police finding out his real identity.

In the morning, Dan could see he was upset and worried. 'Tim, what's troubling you? I know you had a fright last night, but it's more than that, isn't it?'

'I'm scared, Dan,' he answered. 'What if the police take my fingerprints and discover who I am, and want to take me back to Islington and put me into a kids' home?'

'I can see your problem. I'm sending you out with Shep to round up all the sheep and inspect their feet today. It will take you all day. Meanwhile, leave the police to me. I think they will be more interested in whether I have a licence for the shotgun than your fingerprints, son. Eat the good breakfast Daisy's made you, get your coat on, and off you go! I'll come up and bring you sandwiches and a flask at lunchtime.'

Even though it was a lovely spring morning and very peaceful on the hill, Tiago was agitated and worried. The sheep could sense that and weren't very cooperative about having their feet inspected. He couldn't forget the events of the night and fears about the future.

True to his word, Dan appeared at lunchtime with some food and a hot drink. He was smiling from ear to ear. 'No worries, Tim,' he said cheerfully. 'The police just wanted a statement – they know those two guys well. They're always causing trouble. Now they're in custody and they will appear before the magistrates tomorrow and hopefully cool off in a prison cell for a few weeks.'

This cheered Tiago up, and Dan helped him finish the task of checking all the sheep for any foot problems.

'Are you feeling OK about sleeping in the house tonight, or would you rather be with us?' Dan asked as they walked back down the hill to the farmyard.

'I'll be fine on my own,' answered Tiago. 'I have Shep with me, and Sandy – and Shep looked after me last night, didn't he?'

Even though Tiago wasn't afraid of sleeping alone, the incident made him think. If he decided to travel with Dan and Daisy through the summer, he might encounter the police quite often. Dan said they tended to visit the gypsy encampments frequently – some irresponsible gypsies had given them all a bad name and people suspected them of being light-fingered.

Another week or so passed and April showers continued into May. One Sunday morning Tiago decided to go for a walk with Shep. Even though it wasn't so easy to walk in wellies, he put on Dan's old pair, as his were still muddy from working on the farm the day before, and walked up the road towards Dorchester. On the way there were woods and Dan had told him that the bluebells were in bloom and were a sight not to be missed. 'Don't go walking in the woods, Tim,' he told him. 'They're private; but there are lots of places where you can look and see the bluebells from the road.'

He set off in high spirits. Shep always enjoyed a walk and was very well behaved on the roads. The only other users seemed to be a few people out on horseback, also enjoying the morning. At the top of the hill was a crossroads which Tiago crossed so that he would be near the woods and facing any oncoming traffic.

The woods were amazing! Tiago suddenly wished he owned a smartphone with a camera. The leaves on the beech trees were just opening and were a gorgeous spring green, and underneath the trees was a carpet of bluebells. He had never seen anything like it. He loved the smell of the bluebells, too.

Tiago stopped and just gazed at the sight for some minutes, until Shep became bored and started to bark to tell him to get moving. At the top of the road was another junction with a small layby and a patch of grass. Tiago noticed a vehicle in the layby which had been completely burnt out. It was hard to guess what sort it had been – but as he looked he realised it could have been a caravan because of the shape of the twisted, burnt metal. He was just looking at this and wondering, when Shep suddenly barked and disappeared into the woods.

'Shep, come here!' he shouted. 'Stay!' He whistled. Normally Shep was obedient; he was a well-trained sheepdog and by now used to obeying Tiago as well as Dan, but this time he didn't respond at all.

'Sorry, Dan,' Tiago whispered to himself. 'I'll have to disobey you and go after him.'

It was so beautiful in the woods and he didn't want to crush a single flower, but he had to find Shep. He kept calling and calling, and then heard Shep barking. Tiago ran through the trees and found the dog standing by something large. At first, Tiago couldn't tell what he was excited about, but when he came near, he had the shock of his life. Shep had found a body. It was a man, staring up at him with lifeless eyes. Tiago felt sick – then terrified.

'Come, Shep,' he commanded. 'We have to get Dan!'

This time the dog did obey and somehow, even in wellies, Tiago managed to run quite fast along the road and down the hill to the old farm. Daisy saw them coming and called out. 'Tim, what's the matter? You look as if you've seen a ghost,' not knowing how near she was to the truth!

He began to spill out the whole story to Dan while Daisy made him a cup of hot chocolate.

'Slow down, Tim,' Dan said. 'Your words are getting muddled.'

Tiago tried to explain once more about stopping to look at the burnt-out vehicle and then Shep running into the woods and discovering the body.

'This will be a police matter,' Dan said. 'You had best let me wear those wellies and I'll go up there with Shep and I'll ring the police. That way it will look as if I have discovered the body and the police won't have to interview you.'

Tiago stayed with Daisy while Dan trudged up the hill, Shep at his heels. As soon as they reached the burnt-out vehicle, Dan studied it and was sure it was the shell of a caravan. Shep led him into the woods to the body, and he, too, was shocked to see the eyes of a dead man staring at him. He took out his phone and dialled 999.

'Please stay at the site and we will be there as soon as we can,' he was told. It became a long day for Dan. He simply told the story of what had happened – the dog was being taken for a walk and ran into the woods and discovered the body. Dan didn't want to involve Tiago because he knew how afraid he was of an encounter with the police. Eventually, they drove Dan back down to the farm, and left to continue their investigation.

Tiago was so pleased to see Dan. He struggled to get the picture of the corpse out of his mind. It was horrible. He guessed the man might have been murdered!

chapter fourteen

By the end of the afternoon, Tiago had made up his mind. He would have to move on. If there was a murder investigation, then the police would be down at the farmyard again and again, questioning Dan.

'I think I must move on,' he told Dan and Daisy. 'I bring nothing but trouble to you.'

'That you don't,' said Daisy. 'You're a real joy to us – almost like a grandson!'

But together they talked things over, and in the end agreed that maybe he should move on. It would be safer for him. They all felt so sad at splitting up, but promised to stay in touch. Tiago had been living at the farm for more than four months and was like one of the family. Dan and Daisy had grown to treat him like a grandchild and hated to see him take to the roads on his own again, but had always given him the freedom to leave if he wanted to.

'I've something for you,' said Dan. 'Well, actually, a couple of things. I bought a phone for you – it's got £10 credit on it, and there's a card so you can top it up when the credit runs out. Will you promise me one thing? Can you phone us regularly and let us know that you are OK? It would be good to phone each other on Saturdays – but of course, you can contact us any time you want to. I was going to give it to you if you decided to move on. I had a feeling that's what you would decide. I want to give you my Swiss penknife, too. You may find it useful – but only as a tool, never as a weapon!'

'When autumn comes, we'll head back here as we always do. If you're in the area and want to come back and live with us for the winter, we'd love that,' Daisy told him, 'and you can leave your winter gear with us, so that you've less to carry around. It might not fit you, the way you're shooting up, but I'll store it for you anyway.'

'Would you take care of Sandy for me?' Tiago asked. 'I think he'd be more settled. I don't know where I shall end up.'

'Of course, he's one of the family now and he and Shep are inseparable!' was Daisy's reply.

She helped Tiago pack what he needed and stored the other things away. It was difficult for them all to say goodbye. Daisy made sure he had eaten a good meal before he walked back along the road to Weymouth, retracing the way he had walked several months before. His heart was heavy, too. He felt he was leaving such good friends behind; he had grown to love and trust them. However, he knew deep down inside it was the right thing to do. It was time to move on. Hopefully, he would get to live with them when they returned.

When Tiago reached the sea, he sat on the Esplanade and wondered what to do next. His heart sank at the thought of sleeping rough once again. His primary aim was to keep away from the police, so he didn't want to break the law in any way. He thought back to Christmas Day and the welcome he'd received from the church in the town. Maybe he would use his skateboard and skate the couple of miles to the town centre, visit the quiet corner inside the church and say a prayer.

There were people walking in and out of the church, visiting the arts and crafts shop which was on one side, and a coffee shop which was open on the other side. He pushed the glass doors of the middle section which was the sanctuary. Good! It was deserted! He sat on the small bench at the prayer space, a lump in his throat. In the quietness, a question came into his mind. Was the man who had pulled him back from jumping in front of the underground train really telling the truth when he told him God loved him? He decided to take a risk and believe that God was 'up there' somewhere and he could talk to Him.

He whispered, 'God, if You exist and it's true You love me, please help me to know what to do now. Help me find somewhere safe to live. Keep me safe from druggies and sex perverts. Take care of Dan and Daisy and let me see them again. Look after Lizzie, and thank You that she's with Tom and Val. I even want You to help my mum in prison. Make her kick the habit and love us.'

Tiago stood up, then remembered that you had to say something at the end – 'amen' he thought it was – so he decided to sit again and say that. Perhaps God only heard if you said the right words. He really didn't know, but didn't want his prayer not to be answered.

On the table in front of the bench was a pencil and paper to write down prayers. Previously he didn't have the courage to write his requests on paper, but now he felt more confident so he took a piece and wrote, 'God, please help Lizzie, Dan and Daisy, Mum and me. Amen', and posted it into a box. There was still the jar with bookmarks, and a note telling people to help themselves. Tiago thought he'd like another bookmark, so looked through them. He picked out one that had a photo of bluebells on the top and words that read:

> 'I know the plans I have for you,' declares the
> LORD, 'plans to prosper you and not to harm you,
> plans to give you hope and a future.'
> Jeremiah 29:11

Tiago read them over and over. It seemed as if God *was* talking directly to him. He could hardly believe those words could be true, but he hoped, somehow, they might be. He opened his backpack and found the book he'd been given at Christmas – the one about the soldier in Afghanistan who found God was real and could help him.[1] He put the bookmark in it, then left the church. Inside he felt that same, strange peace that had overawed him at the church in London, and a tiny spark of hope was lit within his heart. Perhaps he did have a future and wouldn't be on the run forever.

Tiago loved the harbour, which was only a few minutes' walk from the church. There was a strange mixture of smells – of salt and fish and fuel from the boats – and in his mind was the memory that his dad had been a fisherman. There were plenty of places where he could sit and watch

---

[1] Josh Fortune, *Three Years At War* (Day One, 2012).

the activity around him and eat some of the food Daisy had packed for his lunch. The seagulls swirled overhead, screeching, hoping for a crust, but he now knew better than to feed them. As he sat there he watched the town bridge open to allow several yachts with tall masts to sail through.

Tiago would have been happy to stay at the harbour, but he knew it was a rough area at night-time because there were lots of pubs, so he told himself he'd better move on. Looking at the map which he had got from the library all those months before, he chose to walk along the disused railway track which led to Portland.

A quarter of an hour later he was up on the old railway track. It was a nice, quiet place to walk, with only a few cyclists and dog walkers using it, and it was interesting, too, with the remains of platforms and tunnels. In his mind's eye he could see a little steam train travelling up the track and arriving at Rodwell Halt. A little further on he could just see, hidden among the undergrowth, a sign which read, 'Sandsfoot Castle'. Tiago had always loved castles, so left the track to go exploring.

It wasn't far away, and was a ruin, set right on the edge of a cliff, with gardens behind it. In the gardens, a little café sold hot drinks, and he fancied a cup of tea – he was missing Daisy's brews! Also, to his relief, there were loos as well.

There were only a few people looking at the castle, and as he explored the ruins it occurred to him that he could spend the night tucked up in a corner, protected by the old and very thick walls. He hid in the bushes until everyone had gone, the café had shut and the gates had been locked. Then he slipped back into the ruined castle and made himself as comfortable as he could in the most protected corner he could find. His spirits had sunk when he left the farm and started on the road again, and all kinds of negative thoughts filled his mind.

He woke at first light with the birdsong, but there was no song inside him. He was stiff and cold and missed the hot water to wash when he woke up, as well as Daisy's good cooking.

That day, Tiago wandered around Wyke Regis and Portland. It was OK walking along Chesil Beach, looking at the waves that rolled in and listening to the noise they made, but even the sound of the waves and the undercurrent made him feel very alone and very small. He longed for someone to talk with, or Shep and Sandy to stroke. All the contentment of the past few months vanished, and he felt afraid, vulnerable and lonely.

Tiago bought some food from a small shop in Wyke Regis, and it was there that he saw the local paper, with headlines concerning a murder victim having been found in woodland north of Weymouth. He bought a copy because he wanted to find out what had happened after he had found the body. The sight of the dead man was haunting his dreams and he was afraid for Dan, as he knew gypsies were so often blamed for any crime that happened.

> A body which was discovered last Sunday, by a local resident, Mr Daniel Smith, when walking his dog, has now been identified as Georgi Petrovski, aged fifty. Mr Petrovski, who has been resident in Downend, Bristol, was reported as a missing person ten days ago. Mr Petrovski, formerly from Moscow, arrived in Britain in 1989

and worked in the aerospace industry. He lived alone, and no relatives have been traced in this country.

The preliminary autopsy revealed death occurred around two weeks ago. There were multiple abrasions on the body, which indicate that a struggle may have occurred. The Avon and Somerset Constabulary have now taken over the investigations. Foul play has not yet been ruled out.

Mr Smith, a local shepherd at Hill Farm, was walking his dog near the woods, when the dog suddenly took off, running into the woods. He didn't respond to calls, so Mr Smith entered the woods (which are private property) to retrieve the dog and found him barking beside the body of Mr Petrovski. He then dialled 999 for police help.

The incident may also be connected to the burnt-out caravan found in the layby nearby. The layby and the area in the woods where the body was discovered have now been cordoned off by the police until the preliminary investigation is completed.

Tiago read it through a couple of times. He was so glad that the police had some leads to follow up and hoped that the killer would soon be arrested. It seemed the murderer was possibly in Bristol, and that made him feel safer and relieved for Dan.

He was feeling very lonely and almost phoned Dan, but decided he would try to wait until Saturday, when they had agreed to catch up on the phone. He had mentally to readjust to rough living and coping on his own.

Not really having any clear idea of what to do or where to go, in the afternoon Tiago walked in the opposite direction, away from Wyke Regis and Portland. He passed the Wyke Regis church which stood proudly on the top of a hill, then walked down a road which he figured would lead him back to the sea. He was right in his assumption, but on the way he discovered an old military camp. He was sure it was from the Second World War by the look of decrepit Nissan huts. Some had broken windows and doors open, and the site was surrounded by a high fence and barbed wire. He passed the huts and walked to the Fleet Lagoon, the far side of which was Chesil Beach and the sea. The barbed wire continued on the left side all the way, but at the bottom of the hill there was a modern gate and a couple of new buildings, and notices about it being army property. In fact, a footpath ran all around the army site, and Tiago realised that once it must have been a huge army camp but now was mostly disused.

He looked at the fence and barbed wire, wondering if he could find a way in so that he could sleep in one of the old huts, but in the end decided against this plan because the military might be occupying the modern buildings, so he continued to follow the footpaths along the coast. He passed a farm, but because of dogs barking as he walked by the gate, he thought he'd better not investigate any of the outbuildings. He walked on and came to a place where there was a lane leading inland. It had a proper tarmac surface, which made Tiago think it might lead back to civilisation and he could find a park bench or somewhere like that where he could spend the night.

chapter fifteen

As he walked, Tiago was constantly looking around, keeping his eyes open for somewhere to sleep, and a little way up the lane, set back from the road, he saw a red-brick house with a large wooden building behind and a large, old caravan at the side. There was no car and no obvious sign of life.

Cautiously he looked around, listening for a dog to bark, and when he had satisfied himself that no one was about, Tiago wondered if he could find a way into the large shed, just to sleep that night. He felt scared as he walked up the rough drive as quietly as he could, but he could see that the door was open a little. Aware that once again he was trespassing, he began to shake a little and his heart was racing as he peeped inside the open door. It was a workshop. It reminded him of school – there was a lathe and other tools and machinery, piles of wood and some finished items of woodwork.

One of the subjects Tiago had most enjoyed at school was Design and Technology, and once he had made a wooden fruit bowl which gained him top marks. He loved the feel and the smell of wood and had proudly taken the finished bowl home to his mother. He was so disappointed because she had barely noticed his work, as she was out of her mind that day and high on drugs. He never saw it again. He guessed she sold it for a bit of cash to buy more drugs or drink.

The memories brought back the inner pain and fear as he thought about them. Would he ever be free from them and able to leave his past behind? He wanted to reach into his backpack for something to make the pain go away, but common sense told him a wooden workshop was not the place to burn himself. He was so cold and tired, and his feet ached so much he decided to risk getting out his sleeping bag and blanket and hiding in a corner. He hid in the furthest corner from the door, glad to lie down. Exhaustion took over and he fell into a deep sleep. For the first night since he had found the murder victim, he was not troubled by dreams of the lifeless eyes of the man staring at him.

A man in his early sixties,, even with the eye problem he was currently struggling with, did see him there, but decided not to wake him. He quietly locked the workshop and retired to his caravan for the night.

Next morning, Tiago was woken by the noise of a bolt being drawn and the door being unlocked. He woke with a start when he heard the noise, and his imagination ran away with him. Where was he? Was he in a prison cell? It took a while for him to remember about his long walk which had ended at the workshop. He looked up and saw a guy looking down at him, smiling and holding a mug of tea.

'I guess you would like this?' he asked Tiago. 'You look as if you could do with a cuppa. While you drink it, you'd best tell me who you are and what you're doing in my workshop.'

Terrified, his hand shaking, Tiago reached out for the cup. His mouth was dry, but he managed a whispered 'thanks' as he took a sip of tea. He wanted to jump up and run, but he felt cornered and he was scared. Was this man like Jack? What was he to do? Why on earth had he hidden here? He should have slept under a hedge in a field.

Tiago didn't know, but the guy could see that he was only a lad and wasn't reacting aggressively. He could read the signs. Once he had been housemaster in a boys' reform school, as they were called in past days; a school where troubled teenagers were sent by the Inner London Education Authority. Some were violent and rude, but they had very often only experienced hate and neglect in their lives. Many of them found acceptance and help while they were at the school. This man had tried to teach woodwork to the lads, and there were those who'd flourished under his tuition and become good carpenters and craftsmen. They found the work healing and it helped them to eventually grow into good citizens.

When the guy smiled, his face crinkled up and his blue eyes, even through the thick lenses in his glasses, sparkled. Tiago began to feel a little less scared. The hot tea was so welcome.

'I'm sorry,' he said. 'When I saw the door was open I came in out of the cold. I was so tired and had walked so far that I took out my sleeping bag and curled up. I haven't

116

touched your things. Thank you for the tea. I'll get on my way at once.'

'Not so fast, young man. I'm not chasing you away. I just came over to see if you were alright. I noticed you curled up and asleep last night and decided not to wake you. I don't usually have uninvited guests in my workshop. Maybe you should tell me who you are and what you're doing wandering around the countryside. Why don't you come over to my caravan and I'll cook us both some bacon and eggs?'

Tiago hesitated. Could he trust this guy? He was starving, and the thought of eggs and bacon made his mouth water. He could almost smell the bacon and it was so tempting. The guy had seen him last night and left him to sleep, so he couldn't have too bad intentions, he reasoned. The eyes looking at him seemed to have a kindness in them, and Tiago decided to take the risk.

'Thanks, that's so kind,' he mumbled.

The guy left the workshop and made his way into the mobile home. Tiago found out later that he thought it would give the lad time to decide if he wanted to stay and tell his story, or, if not, he had time to make a speedy exit. He believed in letting young people make choices and in treating them with respect.

Five minutes later, Tiago tapped on the door and the man let him in and told him to sit down. 'If you need the bathroom, it's the first door on the left,' he said to the lad, while he continued to fry eggs and bacon. Tiago was grateful – he did need it. He washed his hands and face and his stomach rumbled as he smelt the wonderful aromas coming from the kitchenette. He was so hungry!

After they had eaten, the guy, who looked quite old to Tiago, but he really had no idea of age, introduced himself. 'Most people around here call me Mr P,' he explained. 'So maybe you could, too. The red-brick house belongs to me, but since my wife died I prefer to live in the caravan. It's not so lonely.'

'Thanks for not chucking me out,' said Tiago. 'My name's Tim Cox, and I come from London.'

'I could tell that, lad. I'm used to Londoners. I recognised your accent as soon as you spoke. I used to be a housemaster in a boarding school and all the pupils came from London. So, what are you doing roaming around rural Dorset?' he asked with a smile.

Tiago felt a little more at ease with the guy. There was a gentleness in the tone of his voice.

'I had to leave my home a few months ago. It was by accident that I came to Dorset. I was given a train ticket which someone didn't need. I had never seen such a lovely place, so decided to stay around,' he answered.

After breakfast, Mr P needed time to think about what he should do. In the past, in his dealings with difficult teenagers, he'd always found that giving them a test was a good way to see if they could be trusted.

'Tim,' he said, 'would you mind doing me a favour? I need some milk and bread. At the top of the lane, if you turn right and continue for about half a mile, you'll come to a newsagent's shop. It would save my legs if you could do my shopping today.' He put his hand in his pocket and pulled out a £20 note.

'Of course I will, Mr P,' answered Tiago at once. 'I'll just get my coat and then I'll go straight away. Is there anything else you need – a newspaper?' he asked, reaching out to take the money.

'That's a good idea,' answered Mr P. 'Maybe you could get the local paper.'

'Yes, sir,' said Tiago and went from the caravan to the workshop and got his coat. He looked at his heavy backpack and wondered. Would the guy go through his belongings while he was gone, or could he leave them? He decided he'd have to leave them, so tidied them up, put his sleeping bag over the neat pile and went to the shop.

It was a fresh morning and Tiago was glad to be outside. The sea breeze blew in his face as he jogged up the lane, stopping every now and then to admire the view over the Fleet Lagoon. The man's home and workshop were in a beautiful location! It was all so different from Islington. Much as he would like to see his sister and his market stall friends again, he never wanted to go back to London to live.

Soon Tiago was jogging back along the lane with the shopping, including the newspaper. The headlines were still about the man who had been murdered. Maybe he would ask if he could read it later. He gently knocked on the door of the caravan and a cheery 'come on in' greeted him.

'Here you are, Mr P,' Tiago said, handing over the bread, milk and paper. Then he produced the shop receipt and counted out the change. He wanted Mr P to know that he wasn't a thief and could be trusted.

'Thanks, Tim,' said the man. 'I'm going over to the workshop now. I don't know what your plans for today are, but if you'd like to hang around and help me, you're welcome.'

'Can I really?' replied Tiago. 'I used to love woodwork at school and I would really like to learn more.'

The two of them made their way to the workshop. Inside, Mr P showed Tiago a bowl which he was hand-carving and gave him a lesson in using the tools. They worked together all morning and the time passed quickly. Mostly they worked quietly together, just Mr P giving instructions when they were needed.

'You know what, Tim,' he remarked, 'I have thought for a long time that now I'm having a bit of trouble with my eyesight, I ought to have an apprentice to learn the trade. I know I don't know you and I have a feeling that maybe you have run away from home, or something like that – but I can see already that you have a feel for the wood. That is very important, and quite a rare thing. You seem to have a natural flair for the work. The way you touch the wood, almost with reverence, is a delight for me to see. I'm just wondering, would you like to stay here and work with me for a bit? I'd have to make proper arrangements, but we could have a month's trial, and if you like it, then we could make it official.'

Tiago was speechless for a few moments. Was he hearing right? Was this guy, who knew nothing about him and his past, willing to offer him an apprenticeship? Then a thought hit him. Did he have ulterior motives? Could he be trusted? Was this seemingly nice guy going to turn out nasty? He didn't have enough experience to know the difference, but he was so tired of running and longed for stability and a normal life. What would Dan think? Maybe he should phone him and ask advice.

'Mr P,' stammered Tiago, wanting to be honest. 'I have nothing except what is in my backpack; no home, a mother in prison; no father. Yes, I would love to learn carpentry – I do love the smell and feel of wood – but I have nowhere to live.'

'I think it's time we went to my caravan and had some lunch and talked things over. It's just a thought and you need time to think,' was Mr P's reply. They tidied up their work and walked back to Mr P's home. It was just a few yards, but slightly hazardous for a guy with poor sight as there were rough patches of ground with large stones to navigate.

Tiago helped him by opening and heating a tin of soup and they ate it with thick slices of bread from the loaf which he'd bought that morning.

'I don't want to be nosy,' explained Mr P, 'but perhaps it would help if you told me a bit about yourself, and maybe we can make a plan.'

Once again, Tiago needed to make a choice and decide if he could trust this man. He thought of Dan and Daisy and how warm and welcoming they had been, even when they knew the truth. He was beginning to sense that Mr P might also be the kind of person whom he could trust, so he began telling a little of his story without giving away too many details that could identify him. He did tell him about living with Dan and Daisy – and finding the body.

'I want to phone Dan this evening and talk to him before I make up my mind,' he added, as he finished his tale.

As he listened intently, Mr P felt sorry for the boy. It was a tale not unlike those he had heard in the past when he had been the housemaster in the school. He knew instinctively that this young man needed stability, and to be in a safe place. He had to be able to trust people again and to continue his education, so that he could make something of himself and one day live his life as a good citizen. He knew, too, he was taking a risk, not in trusting Tiago, but in breaking the rules and not handing the boy immediately over to the authorities, but he felt he had to gain the lad's trust first.

Mr P felt they needed a few days to begin to get to know and trust each other, then he would talk to social services – if he did so at once, the boy would run again. He and his wife had fostered difficult kids after he took early retirement, but would he still be allowed, as a single man, to look after this kid?

'I think we could have an agreement, Tim,' declared Mr P, after a long silence. 'Let's have a month's trial. You can have my spare bedroom or sleep over in the house, whichever you prefer, and in lieu of rent, you can help me with the shopping, cleaning and cooking. In the daytime, I'll teach you carpentry, but in the evenings, we'll do other lessons for an hour or so, after which you'll be free to watch television, go out, or do anything you like. The weekends will be your own free time. How does that sound?'

'I think I would like that,' answered Tiago. 'I promise I will work hard and you won't be disappointed. Can I ask you something?'

'Yes, what is it?' answered Mr P.

'Please may I read your newspaper when you have finished with it, and watch the TV news this evening? I want to learn more about the man who was murdered. I shall feel safer when the killer is caught. At least no one is accusing Dan of anything, but gypsies do get blamed for all sorts of things, just because they are Romany travellers. Dan and Daisy were really good to me.'

Mr P smiled at the lad. He didn't know what he had expected to be asked, but it certainly wasn't just a simple request to read the paper and hear the news!

'I'm interested to follow the story, too,' replied Mr P. 'We'll cut out all the articles from the paper and paste them in a scrapbook for you to keep. One day you may have a family of your own and want to tell them about your adventure, and you'll have evidence to show them.'

'Thanks, Mr P,' said Tiago.

chapter sixteen

Later that day, Tiago phoned Dan. He and Daisy were glad to know that the lad was safe and hoped he would be alright in this new home.

'Is there anything about him that makes you feel uncomfortable? Does he try to touch you in any way or ask very personal things?' Dan asked Tiago at the end of the conversation.

'No,' he replied. 'Funnily enough, he reminds me of a teacher at my old school – always kind and wanting to help you to do well. I don't feel scared and shaky inside any more.'

'It seems you have your answer, then, but still be watchful and careful. Just ring me if you get worried about anything, absolutely anything. You can always come back to us and sleep in the tent. Shep and Sandy will be pleased – they're missing you,' Dan added, before he said goodbye.

After a few days Tiago decided that he could trust Mr P and, having slept in the corner of the workshop, decided he'd move into the spare room of the large caravan rather than be alone in the house, after his experience in the farmhouse, which had really scared him, especially as he now didn't have a dog to keep him company.

'Mr P,' he told him, 'I've decided to take up your offer and come and sleep in the caravan, if that's still alright?'

'Of course it is, but Tim, it won't do to get on the wrong side of social services,' Mr P told him. 'For many years my wife and I worked for them as foster carers after I left teaching. I have already broken the rules by having you here for a few days. I can't risk doing that any longer. I want to ask them to allow me to foster you officially.'

'I'm so scared. What if they don't let you foster me and I get sent back to London? I don't want to be sent into a home and I never want to go back to my old school, and I haven't been totally truthful,' a very shaken Tiago told Mr P. 'My name isn't really Tim Cox. I made that up when I ran away. My real name is Tiago Costa – my dad was Portuguese. He drowned when I was very young, in a fishing accident. I do have a birth certificate and copies of my parents' marriage and dad's death certificates with me to prove who I really am. I lied because I thought I was less likely to be discovered if I used a false name, but please can you go on calling me Tim Cox? I feel safer when that is used.'

'I think of you as Tim, and I'll call you by that name, but I'll have to tell the authorities your real name. Don't worry too much, I have worked for years with the social services and they really want to do the best for the young people in their care and help them into a better life.'

Tiago couldn't help worrying when Mr P rang the Children's Services at the local county council. He was so nervous, with his bags packed ready to run again if the worst came to the worst.

He dreaded the day when the social worker would come to do preliminary visits to Mr P as well as to see him, but still moved into the caravan and felt so glad to be in a home again.

A social worker called Mrs Jennings had been assigned to his case. She called to see him every week to check that all was well, but since he was fifteen, and taking all the circumstances into consideration, and with the agreement of Islington social services department, Mr P was allowed to foster him. Tiago was amazed – he had been so sure that he would be taken like a prisoner to London and shut up in a children's home, but in fact, the worker assigned to him was both understanding and helpful. She found out about his mother and gave him news every week. She helped Mr P get authority to home-school Tiago, so that he could catch up on what he'd missed, and was impressed by his woodwork skills.

Mr P felt happy, too. He felt ten years younger, having a companion and just feeling useful again. He loved to teach, and Tiago was proving to be a bright pupil. Not only did he seem to have a natural aptitude for carpentry, but he was also doing well with Maths and English and the other subjects they were looking at in the evenings.

'I'd like to be able to cook again,' Tiago told Mr P. 'I used to cook for Mum and Lizzie. I had a garden, too, and used to grow tomatoes. I started a garden for Dan and Daisy, too, when I was with them. Can I have a garden here?'

'You bet,' agreed Mr P enthusiastically. 'We used to have one, but I haven't bothered about it since my wife died. There's nothing like home-grown veg!'

It was good to feel useful, and Tiago felt like a million dollars when Mr P praised him and thanked him for his help. The days passed by very quickly and often Tiago found himself singing because he really felt happy and was enjoying his life. Now that the authorities knew where he was and had no problem with Mr P being his foster carer, he felt secure. It was an amazing feeling to know that someone liked you and cared for you and encouraged you, and the feeling of trust grew a little more every day. He missed Dan and Daisy, Shep and Sandy, as well as Lizzie, Tom and Val, but all in all, life, as he told Mr P, was 'well cool'.

At the end of the trial month they sat down together to talk over how they both felt about the arrangement. It made Tiago feel grown up and respected when Mr P asked his opinion. Mrs Jennings, who was a jolly lady in her thirties, was asked if she wanted to come and join in the discussion, and she thought that was a good idea.

'I need to know how both of you are getting on together,' she told them, 'and about your future plans. The school inspector will want to know about your progress academically, too – he monitors all the young people who are home-schooled.'

'Well, Tim,' Mr P said. 'How has this month been for you? Are you happy to go on living here, and learning? From my point of view, it seems to be working very well. I enjoy having you here and teaching you, and you certainly help me a great deal. I think you have a flair for woodwork and you're a pretty good gardener, too. I shall have to take Mrs Jennings out to see all the veg you're growing.'

'Oh, Mr P, I can't tell you how happy I am to have a real home, and I love learning from you. I really want to stay,' answered Tiago.

'I'm glad,' replied Mr P. 'I can't draw up any real legal apprentice document, because you are not yet old enough, but I am happy that we continue in this way and we can review the apprentice situation when you're sixteen – that will be in December, won't it? I do have a concern, though,' he added.

'Have I done something wrong or not done things well enough?' Tiago asked his mentor, feeling fearful suddenly.

'Nothing like that, Tim, don't worry,' he reassured him. 'It's just that I think you should mix and have friends of your own age. You should have a life other than home and schooling. You should be having fun with other kids.'

'I think that sounds a very good idea,' said Mrs Jennings, nodding her head in approval.

Tiago wasn't keen; he had been bullied so much at school, and even the Railway Sleepers' Gang had been into things with which he didn't want to be involved, and he said as much to the two adults.

'What about your skateboard?' Mr P asked him. 'Why don't you go up to one of the skateparks on a Saturday and have some fun?'

'I was thinking about getting a Saturday job and a paper round,' answered Tiago. 'I used to have both in London and that's how I saved enough money to run away. I could pay you rent for my room and food, then,' he suggested.

'If you want a job, that's fine. There's an old bike in the workshop. Years ago, I used to ride it. Why don't we give it an overhaul? It could be useful if you did a paper round. It's a bit old, but then, these days that's an advantage – no one would pinch it! However,' Mr P continued, 'you have to understand one thing. As your foster father I get paid to look after you, so any money you earn is yours to keep, along with the pocket money which I'll give you. We can open a bank account in your real name if you want to save it – but you won't be paying for board and lodging until you are at work!'

A few days later, they cleaned and serviced the old bike, which wasn't in too bad a condition at all. It helped Tiago a lot when he did the shopping for Mr P. One day when he was in the store he asked the shopkeeper if he had any spare paper rounds.

'I'm always looking for reliable youngsters for paper rounds,' he said. 'Many of them only stick at it for a week or so to get a bit of extra cash for something they want. Give me your phone number and I'll contact you as soon as anyone quits. I promise you, it won't be long.'

Tiago was glad that Dan had given him a phone, and now that he was so much more confident, he willingly gave his number. In fact, the shopkeeper didn't need it because Tiago was going to the shop almost every day, and in a couple of weeks he was given a round. He enjoyed getting up early now that the mornings were light, cycling around the roads delivering the papers. It meant he could explore the area, and somehow it made him feel part of the community, knowing he now had an address and properly belonged somewhere.

A special part of each week was Saturday evening. After the football results, which Tiago and Mr P watched together on TV, Dan would phone and tell him all the news. Now that they were back on the road, there was lots of news of the villages where they stayed and times when they met up with their family. Mr P had a map of Britain and together they would find the villages and trace Dan and Daisy's journeys.

Tiago was eventually persuaded by Mr P to go to the skatepark in Portland, and slowly made a few friends among the local lads who regularly skated there. They kept asking him where he went to school, but Mr P suggested that he tell them he was privately tutored. That was a good answer – the other kids were surprised but accepted it without further questions. Tiago just didn't want to tell everyone his story.

Now that the weather had improved, Mr P liked going out. At weekends he walked down to the Fleet Lagoon, where his small fishing boat was moored.

'Do you fancy coming with me and learning to fish?' he asked Tiago one Saturday.

'Wow!' answered Tiago. 'That would be so cool! I've watched the fishermen unload their catch at the harbour, but I've never been in a boat.'

Even with some impairment of vision, Mr P managed well steering the boat and fishing. He soon taught Tiago how to bait and catch mackerel by line, and crabs and lobsters in pots. To do this they needed to row the small boat across the lagoon and climb over Chesil Beach and use the larger boat, which was moored on the pebbles, to fish in the open sea.

The sea was a far scarier place for Tiago than being on the lagoon. The rollers were huge, and he could hear the undertow as they crashed on the shore. The story of the way his dad had died haunted him sometimes when he was out on the open water, but he didn't want to show Mr P that he was scared. The first few trips made him feel quite seasick, but in time he became used to the rise and swell. He grew to long for the thrill of being on the sea and loved the salty, fishy smell of the boat. It only took a few weeks for him to learn the ropes and be a real help to Mr P as they baited the crab pots and lowered them into the water, then collected them in the evenings. They took their catch to a small fish market in Portland, keeping just a few mackerel for themselves.

'I need to teach you how to gut and clean the fish before you cook the catch,' explained Mr P, 'because you need to know how to do the nasty as well as the nice things!'

'I have a knife of my own – a very sharp penknife which Dan gave me,' said Tiago. 'I can use that.'

As always, Tiago proved to be a quick learner and soon got the hang of filleting mackerel and cooking them. Although he had rarely eaten fish before, they tasted wonderful to him, having caught them himself. On good summer days from time to time they made a barbecue on the pebbles. Tiago felt his life was almost perfect – as long as he didn't think about the past. When he did, he felt the same inner pain and fear asserting itself again. It just wouldn't go away, however much he tried to hide it in the back of his mind. There was always a hatred for Jack and a pity for his mum.

He never forgot Lizzie and regularly phoned Tom and Val now that he was fostered and felt secure, to ask how she was. Her birthday was at the end of June and Tiago decided he would like to buy her a present and a card – he couldn't remember either of them ever having a 'proper' birthday with cards, presents or a cake.

'Mr P,' he said one Saturday. 'I'd like to go to town today and do some shopping. Do you feel like coming with me?'

The truth was, he felt like a normal person when Mr P was with him, like he had a family who cared about him. Mr P seemed to understand this, and willingly agreed to go with him by bus to town and do some shopping.

They had fun together buying a lovely doll just right for a three-year-old, some jelly sweets and a pretty card. Tiago was growing so fast that he needed some more clothes and trainers, so they shopped for those as well; then went down to the harbour to watch the world go by as they ate fish and chips. It was a great day. Once back home, Tiago wrapped up his parcel, but suddenly realised he didn't know where to send it because Lizzie was now living with Tom and Val. He decided he ought to phone Tom and ask for their address.

'Hi, Tom, it's Tiago here,' he said, when the phone was answered. 'How are you? I'm ringing because I need your address to send Lizzie's birthday present.'

'Oh, Ti, Val was about to phone yer. We've had some bad news and we need to talk to yer. I'll just get 'er, she's better at explaining than I am.'

Tiago went cold all over. What was wrong? Had something happened to Lizzie? The few seconds while he waited for Val to come to the phone seemed like hours.

Val was calmer than Tom had been.

'Let me explain what's bin 'appening,' she said. 'Like yer know, with yer ma in prison, we're fostering Lizzie – proper – you know, for the Islington authority. I take Lizzie for 'er checks – and the doctor did some blood tests 'cos 'e thought 'er to be looking a bit pale. It's turned out that she 'as a nasty illness – leukaemia. The 'ospital wants to do a bone marrow transplant but yer ma ain't a good match, so they say. She's so sick with them drugs and things – well, she's out of 'er mind, the social worker said, and asked if we could find yer. It could be that yer the only one able to save 'er life. Can yer come back and 'ave a test? I know yer don't want to come 'ere ever again, but Lizzie might die if she don't get 'elp, and yer the best chance.'

Tiago felt a huge lump in his throat. Tears were welling up in his eyes and a huge pain gripped his gut when he heard this news.

'Still there, Ti?' asked Val, in a worried tone.

'Yes, Val. I need to talk to my foster father, Mr P. I need to think. I'll ring you straight back when I know what to do.'

A very shocked, trembling Tiago went into the living room and tried, through his tears, to explain to Mr P what the trouble was. But he couldn't really speak. Mr P waited until he had stopped shaking and then they began to talk.

'I have to go and help Lizzie, but I'm so scared. I can't let Lizzie die. I must go to help her, but I don't want to go back to London. What if they make me stay? I love being here with you.'

'Tell me what the problem is, and let's see what we can work out,' suggested Mr P, so Tiago explained about the illness.

'Yes, Tim. I agree with you, of course you must see if you can help your sister. I'll go to London with you and stay with you all the time. I just need to let the authorities down here know that we'll be away and why,' Mr P said, calmly. 'Would you like me to phone Val for you and tell her that I'll bring you up to London next Monday? Maybe she can arrange the doctor's appointment. It's a good job you have some new clothes to wear – and you can see Lizzie and give her the present. Why, we can even buy some balloons! If you're a good match and can give her your bone marrow cells, it will be the best gift she could ever have – the gift of life! If that's the case, I'll stay up in London and look after you.

'You go and put the kettle on, Tim. We both need a cup of tea. Then you had best phone Dan, so that he and Daisy know what is happening – just in case he tries to ring you and can't get hold of you. We don't want him worried, too.'

Tiago felt much better as he went to make them some tea. He felt so safe with Mr P – maybe that was what love felt like, he thought to himself, this feeling of being completely safe. If so, he hoped Lizzie had felt that when he was looking after her. He had always wanted to keep her safe, but was devastated when Jack had abused her. He felt he had failed. He hoped his blood cells would be right for her and she would get well. Maybe then he could forgive himself that he had failed to keep her safe from Jack.

That night Tiago tossed and turned, sometimes talking to God, asking for Lizzie to get well, asking that they would have 'hope and a future' like the bookmark promised.

chapter seventeen

The next couple of days were busy as they got ready to go up to London. They managed to get tickets through the internet and book a taxi to the station – Mr P didn't drive any more because of his eyesight, but Tiago noticed he still had his old car, tucked away behind the caravan. He contacted some of his friends with whom he had worked when he was teaching at the boarding school. They helped to find accommodation for them near the hospital. Finally, Monday morning arrived, and everything was in place as they set off by train to London.

Leaving the security of Weymouth behind, Tiago felt quite nervous about returning to Islington, but there was an excitement, too. It would be wonderful to see Lizzie again, and Tom, Val and the market where he had had such fun working. Mr P looked so smart, wearing a suit and carrying a briefcase – but Tiago worried for him as his sight was not good and he knew how the Railway Sleepers' Gang often stole bags from vulnerable people. However, he found his friend was far more streetwise than he realised. Once they arrived at Waterloo, Tiago bought the underground tickets and they went on the Northern line to the Angel station.

Leaving the station, he guided Mr P through the streets to the market, where Tom was in his usual place at the fruit and veg stall. It was grand to smell all the familiar market smells and hear the noise and see the bustle!

'My word, Ti,' exclaimed Tom, 'I 'ardly recognise you! You aren't 'arf tall now – a proper man! Sea air must suit you!'

Then Tom introduced them to his new friend, who now helped with the stall as Val was always busy looking after Lizzie, and who would take care of everything while Tom took them to the house.

Lizzie looked so ill, it almost broke Tiago's heart. Had he been right to go away and leave her? Yet he knew that Val was taking much better care of her than he could have done, and she was in a safe place. She gave her brother a beautiful smile and put her arms up for him to cuddle her. She seemed so thin and light, he was almost scared to hug her.

'Oh, Lizzie,' he whispered. 'I love you. I've come back to help the doctor make you better. I've got a present for your birthday,' he added.

Lizzie was so excited as she tore the paper from the parcel and pulled out Tiago's present. She so loved the doll, cradling it in her arms and rocking it. Tiago sat on the floor and played with her while Tom and Val talked to Mr P.

'The appointment at the 'ospital is for tomorrow, I couldn't get it for today,' Val explained, 'but yer 'ave to get permission from their mum, 'cos Ti ain't old enough to sign the forms.'

'Good, I'm glad I've got time to go to the prison first,' replied Mr P. 'I've got the phone number of the social worker who will take me to the prison and ask their mother to sign the form. Fortunately, I have many contacts up here with the police and social services, thanks to the last position I held before I retired. I've also been given permission to take Tim with me so that he can see his mother, if that's what he'd like to do. Hopefully, we can sort all these things out before we see the consultant at the hospital. In any case, as his foster parent I can give permission in these circumstances.'

Mr P asked Tiago to dial the number of the social worker on his mobile for him, as he found it a bit hard to see the numbers and even harder to press the right keys. Soon everything was arranged. They had time for some lunch before taking a taxi to meet the social worker.

Going to the prison made Tiago feel very scared. It seemed such a grim place, even from the outside. They were greeted by a prison officer who had a chain hanging from his belt to which a whole row of keys were attached. He was scary even to look at.

Their names were written in a book before they were told to put everything, apart from the letters that needed signing, into a locker. Then they were given lanyards to wear to indicate that they were authorised visitors, and led into a small room. Tiago was shaking with nerves. He wished he could burn away the pain that had surfaced again inside him ever since he'd got off the train at Waterloo. When his mother was brought to the room by a prison officer, he stared in disbelief. She looked so old and thin. The woman in front of him didn't look like his mum at all. He felt bile rising in his mouth and a deep sense of anger. This woman had ruined their lives. How could a mother do that? Lizzie was now so ill, even though she was being cared for by loving people. Maybe she wouldn't have got ill if she had had better care when she was younger, and he himself could have been dead, for all she cared!

When his mum tried to hug him, Tiago felt his whole body become stiff and unresponsive. How dare she try to hug him! She'd always treated him like a servant, and her boyfriend had done unspeakable things to him and Lizzie!

'Tiago,' she whispered. 'I miss you and I miss Lizzie, too. I hate it here, though I deserve to serve my time. I'm so sorry I let you down so badly. I'm so sorry,' she repeated, tears rolling down her cheeks.

'Yes, Mum, you deserve what you've got. Lizzie and I are better off without you,' he replied. As tears trickled down her face, for a moment Tiago felt sorry for his harsh words – but there was no way he was going to let her off the hook. She had ruined their lives and he felt cold inside when he looked at her; he felt no love at all. 'I'm here to help Lizzie. I'd do anything for her. Then, I'm going home with Mr P. He cares about me and I'm happy in my new life.'

A prison officer escorted Tiago from the room and took him to a canteen, buying him some cola and a chocolate bar. He was upset – truly upset – by seeing his mum, but didn't know how to handle what he was feeling. Different emotions were all mixed together – anger, hatred, pity, disappointment, and the cold fear that seemed to enshroud the building.

While he was gone, the social worker and Mr P explained about Lizzie's illness, and their mother signed the form for the hospital. Then Mr P produced some more papers which his solicitor had drawn up – he explained simply that he wanted to take care of Tiago until he was an adult. He was teaching him carpentry and home-schooling him as well. He would like the arrangement to be legal and for Tiago to become his ward of court – a deeper commitment than just being a foster parent.

'You'll always be his mother, nothing can change that, and I would be the last person to want to take that from you – but you are not able to look after him while you remain in prison and are as sick as I see you are just now,' he said, very gently. 'Don't worry about Tiago – he's shocked and angry. In time I'm sure he'll forgive you. He's a good boy, and a very clever one, too.'

Without any hesitation, Tiago's mother signed the forms, and even thanked Mr P for what he was doing. 'He's got relatives on his father's side in Portugal. One day he must find them. Braga, I think, is where they might still live. Make him understand I am sorry. I am a weak woman. I know I have failed my kids. I'm sorry for that and I hate myself,' she said, wiping the tears that were once again streaming down her face.

Tiago was glad when he saw Mr P come into the canteen, and as they left he felt like he'd been rescued from a horrible place.

The social worker was so helpful and drove Mr P and Tiago from the prison, taking them to their hotel. Once they had unpacked their bags and settled into their rooms, Mr P talked to Tiago.

'Your mother has signed the papers,' he explained. 'One is parental permission for you to donate bone marrow stem cells and have the procedure. The other is one for me – it has still to go through the legal courts, but it is to give me permission to look after you until you are an adult. It legally makes you my "ward of court". I'll still be your foster father, but this means I will take responsibility in every way for you until you come of age. It just means I am totally committed to caring for you. From our point of view, nothing will change – our lives will continue with me home-schooling you, but it does mean that you now have a permanent legal address in Weymouth. I hope you are happy with that. We'll have to go to court in due course, to make the arrangement binding, but while your mother is not able to care for you, I always will. This means you will never have to go into the care of social services.'

'Wow, that is so cool!' replied Tiago. 'You mean I belong to you – not just fostered like Lizzie is by Tom and Val?'

'It's not quite like that – your mother will still be your mother, but I have the authority to bring you up.'

'So, I have "hope and a future"?' asked Tiago, thinking of the bookmark he owned.

Mr P smiled. 'Yes, I guess you do, Tim – as long as you work hard and don't let anybody, or anything, steal that future from you. You have a responsibility, too.'

That night Tiago just couldn't sleep. There were too many thoughts whirling around in his mind. He was trying to take in Mr P's amazing kindness in promising to look after him as a father would. Then he was full of happiness because he had seen Lizzie, and she had found a loving home, too. Then, as he thought about their previous home, he felt full of anger and hate towards his mother and her boyfriend. As if all these emotions were not enough, Tiago was scared about the visit to the hospital. Would the procedure be very painful? Would his bone marrow be a match for Lizzie? Would she get well? She was looking so pale and ill. It was almost 4.00am before he finally drifted into sleep – and then felt awful when his phone alarm woke him at 7.00am.

chapter eighteen

Tiago wasn't used to hospitals, and even the smell inside the building turned his stomach queasy. Once they had registered it seemed a long wait before it was his turn to see the consultant.

'Come with me,' said a nurse in a blue uniform, leading him into a small room. 'Please stand on the scales.' Tiago did as she asked and was measured, then weighed. 'Quite a lightweight, aren't you?' she commented. 'You could do with putting on a bit of weight.'

Tiago thought that she should have seen him before he lived in Weymouth and ate good meals every day! Then he returned to the waiting room until it was his turn to see the consultant.

The same nurse took him into a room where a small lady consultant in a long white coat talked to them. She smiled and joked with Tiago, trying to make him feel less scared. He looked at the trolley by the side of her, which had needles and bottles with different coloured tops. That almost freaked him out. However, the doctor did treat him like an adult and explained a little about Lizzie's illness, and how he might be able to help.

The consultant's assistant then took some samples of his blood, and that wasn't as bad as he'd feared. At least he was lying on a couch and couldn't fall over and faint. He didn't want to appear a wimp! 'You see, I need to do all these tests to make sure you are fit and healthy. I can't take your stem cells from your bone marrow if you have anything wrong with you,' the consultant explained to him.

Thankfully, she made no comment about the scars from the burns on his arms, or other scars where Jack had beaten him from time to time with his belt. At last all the tests were over. Tiago was relieved. It wasn't pleasant, but worth it if he could help Lizzie.

'How long will it be before I know if my bone marrow is a good match?' he asked.

'I'm sending the samples to the lab straight away,' said the consultant. 'You can go home for about a week, while we wait for results, then I'll phone your guardian and, if all is well, you will need to come in and stay in hospital for a few days so that I can take some of your bone marrow. You'll be a bit sore afterwards, but not for long. You are a very brave young man and I hope you can save your sister's life. She's a very brave little girl, too, and we all hope she'll recover and lead a normal life. Now, Tiago, you can get off this couch, but slowly, just in case you feel a bit faint. Nurse Penny, will you take Tiago and his guardian to see the ward where he will stay?' she asked the nurse wearing the blue uniform. Then the consultant smiled at Tiago, saying, 'When you have seen the ward, Nurse

Penny will get you a drink and a biscuit, and after that you'll be free to leave. Ask the nurse any questions that are bothering you. We have all your details. Weymouth is a lovely place to live. I went there for a holiday when I was young and have never forgotten the lovely beach. I'll be in touch as soon as I can.' She shook Tiago and Mr P by the hand, as the nurse opened the door for them.

The corridors seemed endless, but eventually they arrived at Puffin ward.

'This ward has several parts. The main part is for younger boys and girls, with several rooms for children who need to be on their own for any reason. Lizzie will need that after her transplant, so that she doesn't catch any infection, but we make everything as good as we can for them. Then we have two wings – one for teenage boys and another for teenage girls – so you'll have a bed in the boys' wing,' she said, showing them an annexe to the right. 'You won't need to stay long, but for youngsters who do have to, we have a school room and activities room. We're lucky to have this new unit for childhood cancer – it's one of the best in the country.'

Certainly, the ward looked modern and had interesting pictures on the walls. All the kids there seemed to be cheerful and some smiled at Tiago. Nurse Penny took them next into a bright room equipped with games, computers and a huge TV screen. 'Sit yourselves down,' she said, kindly. 'We have a volunteer here today, doing part of her Duke of Edinburgh's Award. I'll ask her to come and make you drinks. I'll be around when you come in for your little op. I'll see you then.' Then she left them alone.

'Are you feeling OK?' asked Mr P.

'I think so, thanks. It's all a bit overwhelming. I'm a bit scared,' Tiago admitted. 'But it's nothing to what Lizzie will have to face, so I can't complain.'

'I'll be with you as much as possible, if you're a match. I'm sure it will all work out just fine,' remarked Mr P.

Just then the door opened and in walked a girl wearing an apron, her blonde ponytail swinging as she came.

She started to speak. 'What would you like…' Then shrieked with delight. 'Tiago! It's you! I thought I would never see you again.'

'Zoe-Ann!' he exclaimed. 'I didn't think I'd ever see you again, either!'

The two teenagers giggled, then Tiago remembered his manners and introduced Zoe-Ann to Mr P.

'He is my guardian and foster dad,' he said, proudly.

'Let me get your drinks and I'll ask Sister if I can have my break with you. I'm sure she'll let me if I explain, then we can catch up.'

A few minutes later Zoe-Ann came in with a tray of drinks and biscuits and sat with Tiago and Mr P in the visitors' room. Tiago excitedly told Zoe-Ann about living in Weymouth and how Mr P had become his foster parent and now his legal guardian, too.

'But what are you doing here in the hospital?' she asked him.

At once, Tiago became sad as he told his friend about Lizzie having leukaemia.

'I'm just hoping my bone marrow will be a good match for her and that she'll get well,' he said. 'We're going back home this evening and the hospital will let me know when the tests results come through. If I do match, then I'll come back here for a few days. Mr P has promised to come with me, so I won't be on my own.'

'Please let me know when you come in. Let me give you my phone number again,' said Zoe-Ann, 'and I'll visit you, too, even when I'm not volunteering.'

All too soon it was time for Tiago to say goodbye to Zoe-Ann, because they had to catch a train home. He gave her his phone number and address, feeling so happy that he could now do that without any worry, as he was now truly safe.

'I'll text you as soon as I know anything,' he promised as they left the hospital building. Zoe-Ann waved them off and her lovely smile made Tiago feel warm inside. Somehow, the thought of coming back to the hospital didn't seem half so bad knowing he would soon see her again.

The journey back to Weymouth was long and they arrived late in the evening. The buses had stopped running so they took a taxi and were glad to be back in their own home, and soon were in bed and asleep after all the excitement of the day. It wasn't easy to settle down to the usual routine of work and study that week, but it did help the time to go by quickly while Tiago waited for results.

Mr P answered the phone the day the hospital Sister rang, and they were so thankful to hear that Tiago was a good match and, if all went well, then Lizzie should have a good chance of recovery. A date was given for him to return to the hospital and Mr P was also told that he would be given a room in an apartment nearby, where parents could stay. That was comforting to Tiago, who was quite scared of going into hospital to stay, although he tried to hide his fear. He sent a text at once to Zoe-Ann, and then one to Tom and Val. He phoned Dan and Daisy to tell them the news, too.

While they were waiting for the results, Mr P had been busy. With the help of his solicitor, the guardianship papers had been completed and they talked together about Tiago's ongoing education. He should soon be able to resume full-time education at school and take GCSEs the following academic year. One evening Mr P sat down with Tiago and asked him how he would feel about going back to school. Tiago went quiet for a while.

'I'm not sure,' he answered. 'I liked the lessons, but was bullied so much that I hated going to school. I'm not sure I want to go back. I couldn't face that again.' He shuddered as he thought of the way he had had to devise different ways of getting home and his great fear of being attacked with a knife. Here, although he had grown, lost his zits and had nice clothes, he still spoke differently from the locals. He'd tried to copy them and speak with a Dorset accent, but it didn't really work.

'Why don't we visit a couple of the local schools and see what you think?' suggested Mr P. 'It might not be so bad down here and you could make new friends. You could go back at the start of the new school year.'

'OK,' agreed Tiago, quite reluctantly.

The weekend after their visit to the hospital, Tiago and Mr P were surprised by some visitors. Dan and Daisy decided to come from Gloucester by train on a day trip. Dan phoned Tiago to say that they were having a day in Weymouth and told him the time the train would arrive.

Tiago was so excited by the thought of seeing his Romany friends again – and he had so much he wanted to tell them!

'Would you like me to come with you to meet them at the station?' Mr P asked him. 'We could all have a coffee on the Esplanade together and then I'll come back home while you spend the day with them.'

'That sounds well cool,' said Tiago. 'I want you to meet them. They're so kind. I'll do my paper round as quickly as I can, and we can catch the 10.30 bus.'

The train was on time and Tiago was hopping up and down with excitement as his eyes scanned the day trippers and holidaymakers getting off the train. When he saw Dan helping Daisy out of the carriage, he ran to them and hugged them both.

'Why, just look at you, Tim,' exclaimed Daisy. 'You have grown so much I hardly recognised you – you're a real young man now!'

'Come and meet Mr P,' said Tiago, taking Daisy's arm and guiding them through the crowds to where Mr P was standing at the station exit. He shook their hands warmly and Tiago could see at once that they liked each other. They walked up the road to the Jubilee Clock Tower and it reminded Tiago of his first day in Weymouth and how amazing it had been to see the sea. So many things had happened since that day!

They found a nice café where they could sit outside and enjoy the sea breeze and the sunshine. There was so much to talk about. Dan and Daisy were living on a common, in a hamlet called Kilcot, about ten miles from Gloucester. Their son had driven them to the city to catch the train and would meet them again late that night when they got back.

Mr P explained all about becoming Tiago's guardian, and how well Tiago was getting on with his studies. They also talked about Lizzie and her illness, and the visit to his mother in prison, before Mr P left to catch the bus home.

Daisy, Dan and Tiago strolled a little along the Esplanade to Greenhill Gardens, where they sat in a shelter. Although they had talked most weeks on the phone, there was so much to catch up with. Tiago wanted to hear all about the antics of his little cat, Sandy, and about Shep, and the places where they had stayed and what they had been doing. Then Dan and Daisy asked many questions about Tiago's new life with Mr P.

'When we come back to Weymouth, you'll still come and visit, won't you?' asked Daisy.

'Of course I will,' answered Tiago. 'I'm so looking forward to you coming back. I may have to start going back to school in September. I don't really want to, but Mr P says it'll be best for me in the long run to try to get my GCSEs. We're going to visit two schools soon. He's promised that if I'm bullied or absolutely hate it, I can leave, and he'll home-school me again. I think I'll have to give it a go, because he's got some problems with his eyesight. He's been so good to me, just like you and Dan. I've been so lucky to meet you all. I could've ended up on the streets big-time and that would've been awful.'

'When you told us about Mr P and we learned he was a good man, we were just so thankful that you had a proper roof over your head and someone to take care of you. Now we've met him, we can see what a good bloke he is. We're glad he's taken you under his wing,' Dan told him.

Then they began to talk about the murder victim Tiago had found in the woods, and he told them how he had kept reports from the papers and was making a scrapbook.

'Who would have thought that we would get caught up in a murder investigation?' Dan remarked. 'It's like a programme on the telly; it's hard to believe it really happened.'

'I think they're finding out more now that they've caught his murderer,' commented Daisy. 'We'll soon learn the truth of what happened.'

There was a café nearby and the three of them had some lunch before it was time to stroll slowly back to the station. Daisy was a little short of breath, so they stopped every now and then and sat on a bench for a few moments. Tiago found it hard to say goodbye at the station, but he was so glad that they had come to see him. He still had his mum and Lizzie, but also now had a whole new family!

chapter nineteen

Soon the date for his return to the hospital was arranged. Special permission had been given for Tiago to donate his bone marrow as he was the only good match that had been found, but he was still a juvenile. Tiago was glad he could help his sister and hoped she'd get well again, but did feel very scared whenever he thought about the procedure. In a way, he was pleased to go with Mr P to visit some schools, because it gave him something else to think about in the days before they returned to the hospital in London.

The first school campus in Weymouth they went to see was enormous. It did have great sports facilities and a sixth form college, should he want to stay after his exams. Everyone was polite, but somehow Tiago didn't feel at home. When he was taken into classrooms, some of the kids stared at him as if he was from outer space. None of them grinned at him or in any way made him feel like they would be his friends. Perhaps they thought he was a foreigner – he'd heard that kids who were asylum seekers had a bad time because they looked 'foreign'. He had a different colour skin to most people in Weymouth, which had become even darker than normal thanks to his being outside so much of the time the past few months. If he opened his mouth to speak he would be identified as a Londoner!

The classrooms and corridors and locker rooms reminded him too much of his old school in Islington. He thought the school had probably been built in the same post-war era, with metal window frames and long corridors, and tin lockers which were now the worse for wear. He had been introduced to people as 'Tim', and he was happy about that as 'Tiago' did sound foreign, and he knew that being different was just not cool in school and made you a target for bullies. Even in the nicest schools he knew that gangs of bullies existed, and although he was now much bigger and probably able to stand up to them, he dreaded the thought of confrontation.

When the deputy headmaster interviewed him, he talked a lot about how important it was to get good GCSE grades, and Tiago was afraid that he might not be good enough as he had spent almost a year out of education. He would also have to give up his paper round because the school was a few miles away and he would need to take two buses to reach the campus.

The second school they visited was nearer the caravan and he would be able to ride his bike to get there. Tiago felt more at ease as he looked around the buildings and campus. The rooms were light and airy with views right over the sea. Kids were chatting to each other and when he was taken into a Year Ten group and introduced as a boy who might join Year Eleven in September, they smiled in a friendly way. The teacher asked where he had come from, and when he told them that his last school had been in Islington, a boy asked if that was near Spurs football ground, and cheered when he said, 'Yes.'

One thing he wasn't prepared for was when the head of Year Ten took him into his study and asked him to do some tests, so that they would know which sets he might best fit into. He was sure he'd do badly, but later in the day he found out that he'd done quite well. That was a great surprise and made him feel that going back to school might not be such a bad idea after all. As they were leaving the premises, Tiago was surprised to hear someone call out, 'Hi, Tim, are you coming to our school?' He looked round and there was Sam, one of the boys with whom he was friendly at the skatepark in Portland.

'Hi, Sam,' he answered, a big smile on his face. 'I'm not 100 per cent sure, but I think I probably will be starting in September.'

'Wow, that's so cool! I do hope you do come – several of us from the skatepark come here and we'll look out for you. Most of us will be Year Eleven next term, what about you?' Sam asked.

'I will be the same year – doing GCSEs. It will be so cool if I already have some friends at school!' Tiago answered.

By the time he and Mr P had returned to the Fleet, Tiago had made up his mind that he would go to that school. They had a place for him and said his general work was well up to scratch. If he worked hard and could pass GCSEs in the essential academic subjects, then he knew he would have better options in his future life.

Once again, Tiago thought of the bookmark he had which told him that God had 'plans' to give him 'hope and a future'. Those words must be true, he felt sure, because it was a miracle that he had stumbled into the farmyard and met up with Daisy and Dan last Christmas, and after that he had found refuge in Mr P's workshop, and instead of throwing him out or calling the police, he had taken care of him and now was his guardian. Then he thought some more. It would seem logical, he realised, that God would also take care of him in the hospital and make sure nothing terrible happened to him.

'Yes,' he decided. 'I'll go back to school and work as hard as I can, so that Mr P will be proud of me and I'll have a good future.'

'I've decided,' Tiago told Mr P that evening. 'I'll go back to the second school we saw, since I'm up to standard and already know some of the boys there. Thanks so much for helping me; I could never have done it without you, Mr P. I'll make you proud of me, I promise, but please will you still help me, especially with woodwork?'

Mr P's eyes shone. Tiago knew he already felt proud of him, and it seemed he was glad he had made such a positive decision.

'Of course I'll help you,' he answered, 'as long as you help me with all this modern technology. I think it's time we both had tablets and computers. And maybe even smartphones? My old computer is so out of date and I'm really quite clueless.'

'Wow! Really?' questioned Tiago, thrilled with the thought of having a computer and tablet to use. He knew it was something his mum wouldn't ever have been able to buy for him.

Going to Dorchester and choosing a computer and tablet did help to keep Tiago's mind off the forthcoming operation, as well as having instructions about using the models and helping Mr P to learn more about computing. He did get time to go to the skatepark at the end of the week and tell Sam that he had decided to go back to school when the new term started in September.

'Yay!' Sam shouted, calling some of the other guys over. 'My mate Tim will be at school with us next year – that's really cool!'

At the weekend, he phoned Dan and Daisy and told them about returning to school. They seemed very pleased for him, too. They appeared to understand how valuable it was for Tiago's future and getting a job.

When he sent a text to Zoe-Ann and told her all the news of the week, she was so excited that she phoned him instead of just texting a reply. How he loved to hear her soft voice! Just hearing from her sent thrills down his body. He couldn't understand why she had always been so kind to him, but he knew that he was really longing to see her again. She promised to come every day while he was in the hospital. She also told him some news, which made him excited and happy.

'Tiago,' she said, 'you'll never guess where we are going for our holidays this year.'

'How can I guess? It could be anywhere. Maybe it's Portugal?' he answered.

'No, far better than that. Dad has hired a lodge on a site on the outskirts of Weymouth!'

'Oh, that's so cool,' responded Tiago, the excitement bubbling up inside him. 'I can hardly believe it. I hope we can spend some time together. Will your parents mind if I meet you and show you around?'

'I've already told Dad and Mum that I have a friend who lives in Weymouth. I'm sure they'll just be pleased I know someone. My little brothers will want to play on the beach – they are still at the bucket and spade stage! Anyway, we can talk about it when I see you next week.'

The school holidays were starting very soon, and Tiago was excited to have something special to look forward to. Mr P had already told him that his home-schooling would stop for a holiday in August, and when Mr P heard about Zoe-Ann's visit he was pleased because he wanted Tiago to have lots of friends of his own age and enjoy as normal a life as possible.

'I'd like to make Zoe-Ann something as a gift,' Tiago said to Mr P. 'Have you any ideas?'

'I could teach you a new technique, Tim,' answered Mr P. 'I've not done it for years, but I used to make jewellery from thin layers of veneers pressed together. Silver birch worked very well as it is soft and flexible. Let's have a look in the workshop tomorrow and see what we can do.'

They loved working together. The age difference between them seemed to just melt away. They both loved the smell and feel of the wood. Tiago soon got the idea of shaving thin strips of wood that were various shades of brown and layering them together with a little glue. Then they had to be held together in a vice. The next day, when they were completely stuck together, Tiago cut out a pear-drop shape, and drilled a hole in the top, then carefully shaped and sanded the sides, to show the different layers of wood. A longer strip he softened in water and then shaped it around a large pipe. That had to be left for another night before he could cut and shape the ends to make it into a bracelet. After that he lovingly sanded and oiled the bracelet. Tiago was delighted with the result! He had put so much effort into making the pendant and the bracelet as perfect as he could. He did hope that Zoe-Ann would like them.

'Wow, Tim,' said Mr P when he saw the results. 'They are brilliant. You could begin a cottage industry doing that, selling them in a craft shop to visitors.'

The day before they were due to go back to London, Mr P sent Tiago to the jeweller in the town to buy a silver ring for the top of the pendant and a chain to go through it.

'Would you like a velvet bag to put it in?' the jeweller asked him.

'Yes, please,' Tiago answered. 'But I need quite a big one, because I've also made a bracelet to match.'

'Did you *make* this pendant, son?' the jeweller asked in surprise.

'Yes, I've been learning the technique this week. I'm going to London and this is a special gift for my school friend there.'

'It looks more like a gift for a girlfriend,' commented the jeweller, and Tiago felt his face go red. 'I'd like to see your bracelet – if it is as nice as the pendant, then I would place some orders with you and try to sell them in my shop.'

'Would you really? That would be so cool! As soon as I'm back from London and fit enough, I'll make some more and then bring them to show you.' Tiago began to explain about the operation he was going to have and that it might take him a while to recover. 'I'll have to ask my foster dad about the wood supplies and how much they would cost, but he did say he thought I might be able to begin a cottage industry with wooden jewellery.'

Having left the shop, with the precious pendant in his pocket, Tiago began humming a song as he walked through the town to the bus stop. He passed the church and decided he had time to pop inside. It had been a while since he had stopped there when running away after finding the dead body and whispering a prayer. He was sure God had answered, especially about giving him a 'hope and a future'.

It was cool and quiet inside the empty church. A wonderful sense of peace swept through him, and a real happiness. He sat and whispered his thanks for all that had happened since he ran away from home. He talked to God about his mother, so ill and in prison, and about Lizzie, that she would get well, and asked for help to be brave in the hospital.

He felt less worried about giving the bone marrow as he left the church and walked to the bus stop by the town bridge. Once again, he hummed a tune as he caught the bus to go home. He felt so happy to have a real home, to really belong somewhere.

chapter twenty

This time when Tiago went to the hospital, although it was to give the bone marrow stem cells for Lizzie, he didn't feel as nervous as he had during the first visit. As soon as he was admitted to the ward, he was able to visit Lizzie, who was already on the younger children's ward and being prepared for her transplant. She didn't understand what was happening, but was so pleased to see him, and was hugging the doll which he had given her for her birthday. She wasn't yet in isolation, so Tiago could hug her and hold her hand, telling her not to be afraid and that he would help her to get well. That made him feel so good just to know there was something he could do to help her. She looked so thin and pale, sitting on a big hospital bed.

Zoe-Ann came to see him in the afternoon as soon as school was finished, and that made him feel amazing. He hoped that their friendship might become special and she would be his girlfriend. He didn't have much experience with girls – but just hearing her voice made his heart beat faster and when she touched his hand, it felt like electricity running all through his body.

'Zoe-Ann,' he said, 'whatever did you see in me to come and sit with me at lunchtimes in school? I just don't understand. I had no friends, and you had lots. I had second-hand, often dirty clothes and zits all over my face. I wasn't good at anything, and my life was a complete mess. I really owe you – if you hadn't come searching the railway stations and found me, my life could be far different from how it is now. I just don't understand why you cared.'

Zoe-Ann sat quietly for a moment, and Tiago could see she did not quite know how to put her feelings into words. Perhaps she didn't altogether understand why she'd cared so much about Tiago and she didn't want to tell him she just felt sorry for him; though he guessed that had been part of the reason.

'Ti,' she answered, 'when we were in the same tutor group, I could see you were enjoying learning, but nobody was making it easy for you. I felt angry that even some of the teachers had a down on you – it wasn't your fault that your clothes weren't as good as other kids' and you couldn't do all the homework because you didn't have access to a computer. That's not fair – those are the sort of things that shouldn't count. I hated the bullies getting at you, because in Year Seven I was bullied so much just because my dad is a vicar. I was called all sorts of nasty names and it really hurt. My dad's like any other person, and so am I. Then, I hated to see you always sitting on your own, and when I went to sit with you your eyes looked so happy, and that made *me* feel happy. I guessed you had a sad story and although I couldn't change that, I wanted to help you get through the day. When we talked together, I

161

didn't see the outside things like clothes or zits, I saw your eyes sparkle, and you were interesting and caring. I knew you were one of the nicest boys in the class and wished others could see that, too.'

Zoe-Ann flushed as she told all this to Tiago, and he was blown away by the revelation.

'You'll never know how much it meant to me, sitting and chatting to you, Zoe-Ann. It got me through the day.'

This chat seemed to dissolve all the tension between them and cement their friendship even further.

Mr P was with Tiago much of the time and had been given a room in an apartment set aside for parents of sick children. Although Tiago wasn't 'sick', Mr P was able to stay there and not have the expense of staying in a London hotel.

'Well, young man,' said the consultant when she came to do her round. 'This is what we hoped for, isn't it? You are a fantastic match and I'm sure that Lizzie will have the best chance of recovery from your stem cells. It's never 100 per cent sure that a person's body will accept the stem cells from another, but we hope that she will do well. Thanks for being brave enough to come and have the procedure. Are you worried about anything or have any questions for me?'

'Do you know what time you will do my bone marrow puncture?' Tiago asked.

'You'll be first on the list, around 8.30 tomorrow morning,' she answered. 'You'll be a bit sore, but you're young and healthy so will bounce back very quickly. If you lived locally you'd probably be going home that evening, but as you live so far away, we'll keep an eye on you for a couple of days.'

All went to plan, and it didn't hurt as much as Tiago had feared. Mr P spent time doing a huge jigsaw puzzle in the day room, and after school Zoe-Ann came to visit him for an hour or so.

The afternoon before he left, he shyly gave her his gift.

'I don't know when your birthday is,' he told her, 'but this is a present I have for you.' He felt himself go red as he offered her the little package, which he had wrapped nicely in tissue paper and tied up with a ribbon. 'Thank you so much for being my best friend – even being nice to me when I was at school here, and everyone else bullied or made fun of me.'

Now it was Zoe-Ann's turn to blush, as she opened her gift. Her eyes lit up when she saw the beautifully crafted pendant and bracelet. Tiago could see she really liked them.

'I've never seen anything like this before, Ti,' she said with delight. 'They are so lovely. Thank you so much. I will always treasure them. You shouldn't have spent your money on me!'

'I didn't,' Tiago told her. 'I made them for you.'

'You made these!' Zoe-Ann exclaimed in astonishment. 'They are amazing! You're a genius.'

Tiago laughed. 'No, I'm not, but Mr P has been teaching me woodwork and he showed me how to make them. When I went to the jeweller to get the ring and chain for the pendant, he liked it so much he's asked me to make some more for him to sell in his shop, so I may have a business opportunity opening up.'

'Wow!' said Zoe-Ann. 'I'm not surprised, they are just so beautiful and special, and no one has ever made me a special present before. I promise, I will treasure them all my life.' Then, she leaned over Tiago and gave him a kiss on the cheek. It was the most wonderful kiss he had ever had. He wished the feeling would stay there forever.

'When you come to Weymouth, if you like, I'll show you Mr P's workshop, where we do woodwork,' he suggested.

'Oh, yes, please,' Zoe-Ann answered. 'I'm so looking forward to coming down and I hope we can spend loads of time together. I know you won't ever want to come back to Islington to live, and I'm glad life is heaps better for you now, but I do miss you.'

It was hard saying goodbye that evening, but at least they knew they would see each other again soon. Meanwhile, they had phones and tablets and there were lots of ways of using them to keep in touch.

The next morning Tiago was up and dressed and everything was ready for him to be discharged home. He wasn't allowed to visit Lizzie, but could wave to her through the cubicle window. She looked so sweet in her Disney pyjamas, clutching her doll. He was sure she would get better now.

There was just one other thing to do before he and Mr P caught the train. He wanted to visit his mum again, and Mr P had been able to arrange that for him.

The prison was such a grim place, and he hated the thought that his mum was there. This time she was in the prison hospital, looking very small in the hospital bed. Tiago could see for himself that she was now a very sick woman. He reached out to hug her and all she could say was, 'I'm sorry, Tiago, I'm so sorry.'

'It's alright, Mum,' he whispered, trying not to cry. 'I've forgiven you. I know it was the drugs and booze that made you like this. I'm alright and things are good with me, and Lizzie's going to be fine. I still love you.'

As they made their way to the underground station, Tiago was very quiet.

'I wonder if I'll ever see my mum again,' he said to Mr P. 'She doesn't look as if she will get better.'

'I truly don't know,' answered Mr P. 'I'm glad you forgave her and told her you loved her. Whatever happens in the future, she and you both need to know that. I'll always bring you up again if she asks for you or you just want to visit. She's pleased that you have a home and are doing well with schoolwork. She told me that.'

It wasn't an easy journey home for Tiago. He kept thinking about his family. Deep inside he felt sure that Lizzie would now get well, but he didn't feel the same about his mum.

Back in Weymouth, Tiago soon recovered from his visit to the hospital and life resumed the normal routine. As planned, home-school lessons stopped for all of August. Mr P was ready to have a break, too. He loved the stimulus of teaching Tiago, and having his company, but he needed a holiday, just as all teachers do.

'Tim,' he said one morning, 'will you take the boat out for me and do a bit of fishing? I know you can handle it well now and this morning I'm feeling tired.'

Tiago was a bit worried. Mr P had been so amazing, teaching him things, coming to London with him. He was aware that his guardian's poor vision made life difficult and sometimes he looked tired.

'Are you alright?' Tiago asked. 'Should you see the doctor?'

'A couple of hours' extra sleep and I'll be fine. I just think you can manage the boat on your own now,' he answered.

Tiago did his paper round as usual, and the shopping. He made breakfast and took Mr P's to his room, to eat in bed.

'Breakfast in bed,' he said in delight. 'Now that is a treat!'

Next Tiago cycled down to the Fleet and then rowed the small boat over the lagoon and secured it on the far side on Chesil Beach. It would be the first time he had taken the larger fishing boat out on his own, although he had helped Mr P lots of times, and he was feeling a bit scared. Fortunately, the sea was calm, but he knew how deceptive the tides could be and that the undertow could be dangerous. Tiago tried to remember everything he had been taught, as he baited the lines and then took the boat out into the deeper water. Gradually, his nerves calmed as he sat quietly in the boat and felt the sea breeze wash over him. He loved the salty spray from the gentle waves and the swish of the waves lapping the pebbles on the beach. The mackerel were biting well and soon he had six big fish in the bucket. That was all they needed – he had been taught to respect the fish stocks and not take more than they could eat.

It was easy to take the boat back to shore, but pulling it well up onto the Chesil Bank and securing it at the mooring was hard work. He laughed as he looked at his developing muscles and tanned arms and legs. How different he looked these days – probably no one in his old school apart from Zoe-Ann would even recognise him! The thought of Zoe-Ann made him tingle. It would only be a couple of weeks and he would see her again. Maybe he could take her out in the boat! That would be cool. The Fleet Lagoon was a shallow seawater lake, and on the far side was a huge pebble bank. It would be fun to row over the lagoon and then climb up the steep bank of pebbles, run down the other side and watch the rollers on the shore of Chesil Beach!

Thinking of her also reminded him that he needed to get on and make some more jewellery for the shop. He rowed back quickly over the Fleet and took the fish home. Mr P was up and dressed, sitting in his chair and reading the newspaper. He smiled when Tiago came in with the fish, congratulating him on a good catch.

'I knew you could manage on your own, especially staying in the shallow waters,' he commented. 'Well done! Those will be the tastiest fish you have ever eaten – your first solo catch.'

chapter twenty-one

After that first fishing adventure, it became part of Tiago's routine to take the boat out once or twice a week, but only in the shallows. He became used to handling it and his confidence grew. It also grew because he was by now working alone in the workshop, using the tools without supervision, and Mr P was spending more time relaxing.

Tom phoned quite often, giving reports of Lizzie's progress.

'She's doin' really well,' he told him, one evening early in August. 'They reckon the transplant's taken well. Poor kid, she's always 'aving blood tests, but she don't grumble about it – if it were me, I think I'd be on the floor. I 'ate needles! A couple more weeks and she'll be 'ome again.' Tiago was delighted to hear this.

Zoe-Ann and her family arrived on the second Saturday in August. Although he tried to be calm, Tiago was beside himself with excitement. It seemed that he had waited so long to see Zoe-Ann again! In the middle of the afternoon he received a text to say they had arrived safely, unpacked and would he like to come and meet the family? Within a few minutes he was on his bike and cycling over to the holiday park. He sent a text to Zoe-Ann as soon as he arrived at the site, as he had no idea where, in the huge complex, their caravan was located. Very soon, he saw her running towards him, her ponytail waving in the breeze. He just opened his arms, and there she was, giving him a hug! It had seemed so natural, so right, and all Tiago's shyness evaporated.

'We're not far from the gate,' she told him, breathlessly. 'The family are waiting to meet you. I'll apologise in advance for Pip and Squeak, my brothers – they are a pain at times.'

'Pip and Squeak?' questioned Tiago. 'What are their real names?'

'Philip is eight and was always nicknamed "Pip". When Stuart was born, he became "Squeak", because before he could talk, he was always trying to copy Pip's words and just made squeaky sounds. The names stuck and apart from their school teachers, everyone calls them Pip and Squeak. They are very nosy, and I'm afraid they'll ask you all sorts of questions. Little brothers can be *very* embarrassing!'

The family were staying in a lodge, not a caravan. It was nicer than the house where Tiago had lived in Islington and was much more modern than the caravan where he lived with Mr P, although similar in layout. There was a lovely veranda at one end, and Zoe-Ann's parents were sitting there having a cup of tea. They welcomed Tiago warmly and were so friendly that his concerns about meeting them and that they might not like him soon melted away. Zoe-Ann went to the fridge and came back with two cans of cola. As they had their drinks and nibbled home-made brownies, Zoe-Ann's parents asked Tiago about his life in Weymouth.

'Please call me Tim,' he said. 'Everyone around here knows me by that name, not that I mind *you* calling me Ti,' he said, looking at Zoe-Ann and giving her a smile. He told them about Mr P, who had given him a home; home-schooled him; taught him woodwork and how to handle a boat, and fish. At this point in the conversation Pip and Squeak ran up, having been exploring. They heard the words 'boat' and 'fish' and immediately Pip announced that he wanted to go fishing in a boat, and Squeak echoed his request.

'It's not my boat,' Tiago told the boys, 'but I'll ask Mr P about a trip. Maybe if your dad comes too, then we could plan something. You'll need life jackets, of course. There are lots of really cool places around Weymouth and Portland which I can show you. Do you like castles? We could have a picnic at Sandsfoot Castle. It's just a ruin, but a great place to play, with a sandy cove nearby.'

Zoe-Ann's parents didn't have any plans about how they would spend the holiday, so were happy to have suggestions from Tiago.

'We'd like to go to church tomorrow,' said Zoe-Ann's mum. 'Have you any ideas where would be best to go?'

'I've only been in one church, and that's the one in the town centre. There are car parks nearby and the people are very friendly. I had Christmas dinner with them when I was living rough. It's near the beach and harbour, so you can easily find it.'

'Thanks, Tim,' answered Zoe-Ann's dad. 'I think you'd better start calling us Richard and Jo, since we'll be seeing quite a bit of each other this holiday. We've been praying for you for a long time, even before you left Islington. I hope you don't mind that, but Zoe-Ann had told us one of her classmates was having a hard time and being bullied a lot. Then she kept us up to date when she learned you were safe in Weymouth. It's good to meet you at last, and we hope you will be friends with the whole family as well as with our daughter.'

It was a good start to the holiday and Tiago did see a lot of the family during their stay. He just wanted to be with Zoe-Ann as much as possible, but as he got to know her parents and brothers, he enjoyed being included in their family life. He just wished Lizzie was with them, then it would have been perfect.

Near the beginning of their stay, the family all came out to meet Mr P and to see where Tiago was living. The boys had to be kept firmly under control when they were shown around the workshop, but Richard was really interested in all the machinery. He'd been very impressed by the pendant and bracelet Tiago had made for Zoe-Ann, which she wore almost all the time when not at school. At the end of the day, Tiago barbecued mackerel for their supper and they had a picnic on the field behind the workshop. Jo was impressed with his culinary skills, but even more impressed with his care of Mr P, whom it was obvious he really loved.

Tiago spent one day alone with Zoe-Ann, rowing her around the Fleet Lagoon and having a picnic on Chesil Beach. They swam in the lagoon, which was safer than on

Chesil Beach, because of the dangerous undertow. She looked so beautiful in her bikini and, as they lay side by side on their towels, letting the sun dry their skin, he found his hand touching hers, gently. She didn't pull away but turned her head and smiled at him. Their eyes locked momentarily. Electricity seemed to flash between them, and they both knew that their friendship was special. Tiago wanted the moment to go on and on, but the tide was on the turn and he knew he needed to row safely back to the other side. He also felt very protective towards Zoe-Ann and was aware that he must keep his emotions in check. She was one very special girl!

'It's very calm this morning,' Mr P announced at breakfast one day. 'Why don't you phone Richard and Jo and see if everyone would like to come mackerel fishing?'

An hour later the family arrived, complete with food for a picnic. Tiago rowed them in relays over the Fleet and Mr P showed them all how to bait the lines for fishing. Pip and Squeak loved fishing and became very excited when they caught some mackerel.

'Can we eat them for supper?' Pip asked Mr P, and, as usual, Squeak echoed the request.

'No problem,' smiled Mr P, who seemed in his element surrounded by young people. 'We'll make a fire on the beach and roast them on the coals.' It was magical to have a picnic on the beach at the end of the day.

On carnival day they all went to Weymouth to take part in all that was happening, staying to watch an aerobatic display of vintage aircraft before they headed back to their campsite. Later that evening, after supper, they all went down to Sandsfoot Castle to watch an amazing firework display over the bay.

'I wish we could stay here forever,' Zoe-Ann whispered to Tiago, as they stood close together holding hands, with fireworks exploding in the sky.

'Me too,' said a loud voice behind them. 'Do we have to go back to London, Dad?' Pip asked. 'I want to stay here!'

'And me, why can't we stay and live here?' echoed Squeak.

'Don't be daft,' Zoe-Ann told them. 'Dad and Mum have to go back to work and we have to go to school. Holidays always have to end.'

'I'm afraid Zoe-Ann's right,' laughed their dad. 'It's back to work on Monday for me. At least Mum has a bit more holiday, but when September comes, everything will return to normal. Just be thankful for the fantastic time we've had – and not a day of rain. Without Tim and Mr P we wouldn't have had half the fun we've enjoyed. Maybe we can come again next year.'

Tiago knew that it would be hard to say goodbye to this family, but especially to Zoe-Ann. However, on the very last day, something happened which took his mind off the situation.

chapter twenty-two

On the last day of Zoe-Ann and her family's holiday, Tiago woke up early. He wasn't sure why, but he sensed something wasn't right. He got up and put the kettle on; he usually had a hot drink before he did his paper round. He had intended to do the round early so that he could go with his friends to church. He wanted to spend the last day with Zoe-Ann and her family. He knew he would miss them when they went home.

Soon the tea was brewed. Tiago poured out a cup for Mr P and gently knocked on his door. There was no audible answer, so he quietly opened it and crept in. To his utter horror, he saw that Mr P had fallen out of bed and was in a heap on the floor. Panic came over him. He put the tea on the bedside table and knelt down beside his foster dad, praying that he wasn't dead. He felt a bit cold, but much to his relief, he was still breathing.

'Mr P,' he called. 'It's me, Tim. Wake up! Oh, please, please wake up and talk to me.' There was no response. In his panic and fear, his mind wouldn't function properly. What should he do?

Then, in a moment of clarity, Tiago pulled the duvet from the bed and wrapped Mr P in it to keep him warm, then went running for his phone. He dialled 999 and, thankfully, the response came quickly. Struggling to keep his emotions under control, he answered the questions the operator was asking.

'Stay calm and sit with your dad, and listen for the ambulance's siren. Then open the door,' he was told. 'They should reach you within ten minutes, but phone back if you see any changes before they arrive. Have you someone you can phone who will come and be with you?'

It was a relief to be told what to do, and he phoned Zoe-Ann at once. A very bleary-sounding answer came back. Zoe-Ann was more than half-asleep.

'Whatever is it, Ti?' she asked. 'What's wrong?'

'It's Mr P. I just found him on the bedroom floor. I don't know what's the matter – I'm so scared. He's cold and sweaty, but he's breathing. He's not answering me when I talk to him. The ambulance should be here soon – I rang them about ten minutes ago. I'm so scared he'll die.'

'Ti, I'm going to wake Dad and ask him to bring me round. If you've gone to the hospital, do you know which one it will be?'

'The main hospital is in Dorchester. That's the nearest A&E. I'll text you when I know more. Must go and open the door. I can hear the siren, thank God.'

The paramedic and ambulance driver took over. They were talking to doctors in the hospital and he could tell they were concerned. Tiago sat beside his foster dad, holding his hand and hoping that he would recover.

It was scary in the A&E department. The nurses met the ambulance and they rushed Mr P into a cubicle, asking Tiago to sit outside and wait, and they would come and find him to get Mr P's details once the doctor had done his initial assessment. He felt so alone – so scared! The old pain inside seemed to hit him; he had a knot in his stomach. Much to his embarrassment a tear or two started to roll down his cheeks. He tried to wipe them away. He told himself that he was almost a man,; he must be strong for Mr P.

Tiago felt a gentle touch on his arm, and there was Zoe-Ann. He looked up at her and the tears just ran down his face. She held him in a hug and let him cry. Richard stood beside her, and when Tiago had composed himself a bit, he said, 'Tim, we're here for as long as you need us today. Has anyone told you what is going on and what Mr P's problem is?' Tiago shook his head. 'OK, then, I'll see what I can find out.' Richard strode over to the nurses' station.

'Dad will find out. He's a vicar and is used to these situations. Let him talk to people for us,' said Zoe-Ann. 'Thanks for phoning so we could be here. I'll stay with you as long as I can. I wish we didn't have to go back to London tonight.'

'I just don't know what I would do if anything happened to Mr P,' Tiago told her. 'He's been amazing to me. He's helped me get my life back on track. I was so scared of trusting him when I first met him, but now, he's like a real dad.'

Soon Richard arrived with a cardboard tray, three cups of tea and a packet of chocolate biscuits. He smiled as he handed them round.

'I've had a chat with the nurse. It looks as if Mr P may have fallen out of bed and have a bit of concussion. Thanks to you finding him so quickly and getting him here, he should have a good chance of recovering well. He's conscious now and has been able to answer the doctors and nurses' questions and give them the information they need. Soon you'll be able to sit with him, Tim, and they hope to transfer him to the medical ward as soon as they have a single room. Meanwhile, when we have had our drinks, why don't we just slip into the chapel and pray for Mr P?'

The chapel was quiet after all the noise in the A&E department. Tiago wasn't sure what to do; should he kneel down? He felt very shy in front of Richard. He had no idea what being a vicar really meant. He thought that ministers were very holy people and yet Richard did seem just an ordinary person, and they'd had a lot of fun together over the past couple of weeks. Zoe-Ann sat quietly on a chair, closing her eyes, so Tiago copied her. Then Richard sat with them and just talked to God out loud, in a very ordinary way, just as if he was talking to a friend in the room, asking that Mr P would be comfortable, have the best treatment and quickly recover. It somehow surprised Tiago that you could talk to God in the same way that you talked to your friends.

When they went back to A&E, Tiago was able to sit with Mr P until he was taken upstairs to the ward. He had a drip in his arm and an oxygen mask over his face, which was quite scary to see, but he was conscious and smiling and squeezed Tiago's hand reassuringly. Once he was settled in a side room on the ward, the staff suggested that Tiago went home, because Mr P needed lots of rest. He could come back to visit between six and seven that evening. The staff had his phone number and promised to call at once if there was any change in Mr P's condition.

'Good job we're here to take you home,' said Zoe-Ann. 'Saves waiting for a bus.'

'I think the best thing to do is to go to the lodge and have some lunch together,' Richard said. 'Then I'll run you home, Tim, before we start back to London.'

'Thank you so much, you've been so kind. I hope I've not spoilt your last day down here,' said Tiago, as they drove back to Weymouth.

It was very hard to say goodbye to Zoe-Ann and her family after lunch, but she promised to text as soon as they arrived back in Islington, and Tiago promised he would phone with news of Mr P after the evening visiting.

Tiago packed a bag with pyjamas and washing things for Mr P and cycled up to the hospital in the evening to visit. He was so encouraged to see that Mr P was propped up in bed, looking much better. Tiago didn't stay very long because he could see that Mr P was finding it hard to stay awake.

Before Tiago went home, he told the Ward Sister, 'He's been rather tired recently – he's been working so hard, home-schooling me and preparing lessons. He doesn't see all that well, so it's hard work for him.'

'Yes, he's told us about that and I want to arrange for the eye specialist to see him while he is in hospital. I think something might be able to be done to improve his sight,' the Sister answered.

'Wow, that would be so cool,' Tiago exclaimed. 'He struggles a lot and I worry when he uses the machinery in the workshop. I try to watch out for him and will do everything I can to help him get better.'

'Yes, he's been telling me about you, Tim. He's so proud of you. We've had to inform social services that he has been admitted, since you are fostered. Your social worker has promised to come and visit you this evening after visiting is over.'

Tiago froze for a moment when he heard those words. Was it all going to begin again, the uncertainty, the fear of being taken into care? The drumming began again in his head as the old rhyme went through his mind, 'Run, run, as fast as you can!' He fought the fear as he felt his stomach churn.

'I had better ride home, then,' he said to the Sister. 'I need to be ready for Mrs Jennings' visit.' In his head he was thinking, 'Maybe I should be away before she comes.'

It was a sultry summer's evening as he rode down the ridgeway and into Weymouth. He knew the roads well and rode through the outlying villages to get to the Fleet. The countryside around him calmed his fears a little and helped him to think more clearly. Perhaps Mrs Jennings just wanted to see if he could manage on his own for a few days – he was only a few months from being sixteen, not five years-old as he had been when he went into care as a small child.

He'd just arrived back in the caravan when he saw a flash of lightning, which was followed by a loud crack of thunder. On the caravan roof he heard the screech of the seagulls – they didn't like the storms, and if he was honest, neither did he. The sky was dark, even though it was only just eight o'clock, and the rain began to lash against the caravan. Although it was fixed permanently to the ground, it began to sway. Tiago felt very alone and a bit scared and was glad when he heard a car pull in and heard a knock at the door. He let Mrs Jennings in quickly because the rain was so hard that she could have been drenched in just a few moments on the doorstep.

'Thank you, Tim,' she said, gratefully, as he led her into the lounge. 'Could you make me a cup of tea? I hate thunderstorms, and it is very wild down here by the shore.'

'Of course, Mrs Jennings, I won't be a moment,' answered Tiago, as he sped into the kitchen. He soon came back with a tray with two cups of tea and some biscuits.

'You must know why I am here,' she said to him, sipping her tea. 'The hospital had to let me know that Mr P had been admitted, because you are in foster care. I've been making plans this afternoon and although I know you are quite capable of looking after yourself and everything here, it's a very lonely and wild place to stay on your own, especially at night and in stormy weather. I remember you telling me about the unpleasant experience you had when you were little and taken into care. Being snatched away from your mother as a small child would always leave bad memories, because you would feel abandoned and not understand what was happening. Now you are a sensible young man, and although you would rather stay here, Mr P would be worried and that won't help his recovery, so this is what I have arranged.'

Tiago's heart sank and in spite of trying to be in control, he began to shake a little. After a few sips of tea, Mrs Jennings continued.

'There's a very nice couple, Mr and Mrs Hall, who have fostered many young people in emergencies for us, and they are happy for you to stay with them for a few nights. They have their own son, who is in his thirties and has Down's syndrome, living at home, but he is a lovely guy who enjoys visitors. They live in Chickerell, so are very near. You can continue to do your paper round. In fact, they're happy for you to come down here, make sure everything is OK and work in the workshop as well as visit Mr P as often as you can. Basically, they're just providing a safe place to sleep and making sure you get a good breakfast and evening meal. Are you happy about that?'

Tiago felt a little bewildered but realised that Mrs Jennings had done the best she could for him, just doing her job and keeping him safe. He agreed to go with her, still somewhat fearful, but knowing that it would help Mr P to rest and not worry about him if he did as Mrs Jennings suggested. He asked if he could make a couple of phone calls before they left, and Mrs Jennings agreed.

His first call was to Zoe-Ann to update her on Mr P's condition and his move into care for a few days. He tried to sound upbeat about it – but she wasn't deceived and promised she and the family would keep in touch every day and also pray for him and Mr P. Then he called Dan to let him know what was happening, and finally Tom and Val.

'Don't yer worry too much, lad,' Tom told him. 'We love 'aving Lizzie to look after. I bet you'll get folks who'll love 'aving you around.'

That thought cheered Tiago up and he threw a few essentials into his backpack and locked up the caravan. Mrs Jennings took him to the Halls' home and introduced them. Guy, their son, wanted to shake his hand and make friends. He had a lovely smile and it helped Tiago to relax.

'I'll call you tomorrow, Tim,' Mrs Jennings said as she left. 'Any concerns, ring me and I'll be along to see you.'

Supper was on the table and his hosts asked him to call them Bob and Lorna. They seemed pleased to have him and very concerned to hear about Mr P and his illness.

'I met your foster father and his wife some years ago at a party for foster parents,' Bob told him. 'Such a lovely couple and we were very sorry to hear later that he had lost his wife. He used to do lovely woodwork. Does he still do it?'

Tiago began to tell them about the workshop and how Mr P was teaching him, and one day he hoped to be his apprentice. By the time they had finished chatting and he had been shown his bedroom and unpacked his few belongings, he felt reassured. His fears about being in care seemed to be unfounded.

chapter twenty-three

Even though the Hall family were kind, it was lonely for Tiago while Mr P was in hospital. After breakfast he went to the caravan and kept himself busy in the workshop and garden and doing little jobs around the place. He was missing the company of Zoe-Ann and her family, too. They'd had so much fun together over the last two weeks. Tiago phoned her every evening when he came back from visiting, to update her on his news. He just loved to hear her voice, it always cheered him up.

One morning, after doing his paper round, he decided to go to the skatepark, hoping to see if Sam and the others were around, and have some fun; but the boys he knew were not there, so he didn't stay for long. It made him feel lonelier than ever.

Then at supper that evening, Guy asked him, 'Please, Tim, can I come with you and work in the garden? I know how to – I help Dad in ours.'

Tiago hesitated for a minute – then remembering what it was like to be wanted and not ostracised because you were different, he answered, 'Sure, Guy, but I'll be staying there all morning. I'll walk back with you before I go to visit Mr P in the afternoon. Is that OK?' The smile on Guy's face made him realise it was more than OK, and Mrs Hall made them both sandwiches for lunch.

Tiago was quite possessive about his garden and very proud of the way it was looking and producing, but he needn't have worried that Guy might spoil it, for he was a natural, quickly getting stuck into the weeding, which needed tackling. Tiago went into the workshop and began working on his jewellery. He could hear Guy singing outside and was glad he was happy, and so invited him to go with him any morning when he went to work. It was good to have company and he felt less lonely.

Mr P was soon feeling much better, but had to wait a day or so to see the eye specialist. One afternoon when Tiago arrived to visit, he could see that his foster dad was very excited.

'Tim, tomorrow I'm having an operation on my eyes, it's quite experimental, but they hope to restore a lot of my vision,' he told him. Tiago felt excited, too – it seemed almost too good to be true! 'Don't come to visit tomorrow, because after the operation I have to lie flat and keep still for twenty-four hours. But pray it goes well; there's a danger not only of it not working, but that I could lose my sight if it goes wrong. It's a very small risk and I'm willing to take that, but it's a bit scary when you think about it too much.'

'Maybe I'll tell Guy we won't go to the caravan tomorrow and I'll go to town and to the church to pray. I'll ring the ward and see how you are in the afternoon and be in to see you the next day,' Tiago answered. As soon as he was out of the hospital he rang Zoe-Ann and asked her and her family to pray. He knew they all prayed together each evening and felt they knew much better how to talk to God than he did.

Tiago phoned the ward the next day and was told that the operation had gone well, and they had every hope that it would make a difference to Mr P's sight. What relief he felt; his stomach had been a knot of fear all morning, even though he had gone as planned to the church and prayed as he'd promised.

When the bandages were taken off the next day, although his eyes looked black and blue and swollen, Mr P could see more clearly than he'd done for years. It was a miracle! The rare condition, the name of which Tiago couldn't pronounce, used to be untreatable, but research and new techniques had changed that. Within two days Mr P was allowed home. The only person who seemed sad was Guy; he'd loved coming to help with the garden.

'Why don't you come down twice a week and I'll pay you to be Tim's helper?' suggested Mr P. 'Tim will be going back to school very soon, and won't have so much time for the garden. He'd hate it all to get as untidy as it used to be before he took it over.'

Guy was thrilled. He had a job, a real job! It was so much better than going to the day centre where he had to do things he wasn't interested in. His smile almost stretched from one ear to the other! Tiago was pleased, too. He hadn't thought about how much less free time he would have once he was back in school, and he did want to keep his jewellery business going. He liked to see Guy so happy and hear him singing in the garden.

Mr P had to take it easy for a few more weeks, but with his eyesight improving every day, he was able to read more and began to enjoy using his new computer.

The new school term was soon to start, and their routine would have to change.

'I want you to give up your paper round now,' Mr P told him. 'Helping me until I'm really fit, going to school, doing homework or woodwork is more than enough for you. Guy is helping with the garden and you need to have some fun!'

Tiago was quite worried about returning to school after almost a year's absence, but it wasn't as bad as he thought it might be. Sam and his friends were true to their word and introduced him to their classmates. He had grown so tall and looked so different from the way he had a year ago in Islington. He needn't have worried; nobody bullied him at all. Most thought he was some sort of hero because Sam had told most of the year group that Tim had given his bone marrow to help his sister get well and made fabulous wooden jewellery.

'I've been told that you make wooden jewellery,' the Design and Technology teacher said to him in class one day. 'Why don't you bring samples of your work to show the class?'

Tiago did, and they were admired. He found the girls were often around him and wanting to chat him up, but he wasn't interested. Zoe-Ann was the only girl he cared about. When the girls asked him to make them necklaces or bracelets, he just directed them to the shop in Weymouth where they could buy them.

'What's the matter with you?' Sam asked one day. 'All the girls are crazy about you and say you are the coolest guy in the year, but you don't want to know.'

'My girl is in London, at my old school,' Tiago told him. 'We get to talk every night. Her name's Zoe-Ann, and she's the only one I make jewellery for.'

There were some subjects where Tiago was still a bit behind the rest of his classmates, but he was a hard worker and was now enjoying school, and even homework, so began to catch up. In other subjects, he was well ahead and thanks to Mr P's tutoring, he was placed in the top set for most subjects. He smiled to himself: who would have thought that school could actually be enjoyed?

By the half-term holiday, Mr P was completely better, and his eyesight was amazing, so the pair decided to go to London for a few days, as Tiago wanted to see Lizzie and Zoe-Ann. They intended to stay at a hotel, but once Zoe-Ann heard of the plans and told her family, her mum insisted that they stayed at the vicarage.

It was huge fun going back to the market and chatting to Tom, then going to their house to see Val and Lizzie. Lizzie was getting better, but still had to take drugs every day to stop her body from rejecting the transplant. Her immune system was becoming stronger and Val hoped that soon she'd be able to go to playschool and have fun with other children. Tiago had made his sister a whole set of wooden bricks, which she loved. They played together with them, and he could see how happy she was. It was so good to see her smiling and laughing all the time.

Then they took Tiago aside and spoke to him seriously.

'The social worker comes every week, Tim,' said Val, 'and she told us yer mum's been diagnosed with pancreatic cancer and there's nothing that can be done to cure 'er.'

Tiago was very quiet as he tried to take in this news. He didn't want his mum to die. He didn't really know what he felt; it was just a sort of numbness inside. He had loved his mum, but it had been a long time since they really talked together or had a proper mother and son relationship. Alcohol and drugs had robbed her of her mind years ago.

'She told us that yer mum said she'd like yer both to be adopted by yer foster parents if that's what they want, and 'as put it in writing. We want yer to know that of course we'll say yes when the time comes – and yer'll always be welcome to come and be with yer sister.'

'Thanks, Val, I'll always love my little sis, and I never want to lose touch, not ever,' was Tiago's fervent answer.

While Mr P visited old friends in the city, Zoe-Ann and Tiago had outings together. Tiago had seen some of the sights of London, but wanted to see them again and visit other ones, so they visited places like the Tower of London and Buckingham Palace. A couple of times they took Pip and Squeak out to the local park because they now thought of Tiago as a sort of big brother and wanted him to play football with them.

Just before they went home, Mr P took Tiago once again to see his mother, who had now been transferred from prison to a hospice in east London.

'You understand this will be a goodbye visit, Tim,' Mr P told him. 'She has terminal cancer and only a very short while left to live. I was talking to Lizzie's social worker at Tom's house, who said that your mum can barely speak now, and maybe won't recognise you. I told her and Tom and Val that I knew you would want to see her, even for a few minutes.'

Tiago had no idea what to expect in a hospice. He was surprised that it didn't smell like a hospital, and his mum was in a nice room with pretty curtains and bedspread. Everyone was speaking kindly about her, as if she was an ordinary person, not a criminal transferred from prison. He was able to sit next to her and stroke her hand. There was a moment when she did open her eyes and smiled at him, then closed them again.

They didn't stay for long, but as they got up to leave, Tiago leaned forward and gently kissed her forehead. 'Goodbye, Mum, and God bless you,' he whispered. 'I love you and so does Lizzie. We are both good and being cared for.'

As they walked back to the underground station, suddenly Tiago realised that maybe he would have to see to things for his mum after her death.

'What happens after someone dies?' he asked Mr P. 'I mean, how do we get her buried and things like that? She's only got me to look out for her.'

'That's one of the things I tried to arrange when I went to the City. My solicitor is one of my long-standing friends I visited yesterday, after I had learned how sick your mother is. She may only have you, but I'm responsible for you, and so I'll see that everything is done properly. I talked to Richard and he is willing to help with this. We will arrange for your mum to be cremated and then the ashes can be buried or scattered somewhere where you think she would like to be. It's hard to talk about death and make these decisions, that's why we're here to help you. Just think a little about it and when the time comes, we'll know what to do.'

The time came very soon, much sooner than Tiago had expected, but then, he didn't have any experience about such things. He and Mr P had only been home for a few days when the news came that his mum had passed away peacefully in the hospice. After Tiago had talked to Zoe-Ann that evening, Richard came on the phone and told him that he would make all the arrangements at the crematorium and be willing to take the service. Mr P had already promised to take care of all the bills, as his mother had died penniless.

Tiago still didn't know how he felt. Sometimes he felt angry and sometimes he felt a deep pain in his stomach. Mr P was wonderful. He informed the school of what had happened and took Tiago back to London for the cremation. Only a few people had come to say goodbye to his mother. He wore his school uniform, Mr P beside him in his dark suit. Then Zoe-Ann and her mum sat behind them. Just before the service began, two of the hospice nurses arrived, and then Val and Tom.

Richard walked in front of the coffin, on the top of which was a lovely bouquet of pink roses with a card which said, 'With love from Tiago and Elizabeth.'

Tiago couldn't remember much of what Richard said, except that he read Psalm 23 about the Lord being the

Shepherd, and then they sang about it, and he reminded them all that God loved every person very much. That bit stuck in his mind.

After the little service, they left the chapel, and Zoe-Ann came over and held his hand. When she did that, suddenly his eyes were full of tears, and great sobs seem to come from somewhere very deep inside him. Zoe-Ann quickly led Tiago to a quiet corner where they were out of sight, and he buried his head in her shoulder and sobbed and sobbed as she held him. He cried for the mum he remembered when he was very young; then for the woman she had become in later years, so addicted, so sick; he was so sad for the mum he had wanted her to be and for the mum she just wasn't able to be.

At last the tears were spent.

chapter twenty-four

Tiago found it difficult to get on with his life after his mum's death. He hadn't realised how deeply he had loved her, even though so many bad things had happened. He felt as if there was no anchor in his life, knowing that he now had no parents; he was orphaned.

He did his best to work hard at school and in the workshop, but something of the spark had gone. His lifeline was to talk each evening to Zoe-Ann. He could feel the kindness in her voice, and it was this that kept him from beginning to self-harm again, but it only kept the pain inside away for a little time. Mr P was worried. He tried to arrange treats to take Tiago's mind away from his grief, but as the days became colder and winter arrived, it was less easy to get out and about. The boat had been put away for the winter, and for days the Fleet and Portland seemed to be shrouded in a thick sea mist, which matched his foster son's spirits.

Mr P had a bright idea one Saturday morning. 'I've always wanted to go to Yeovilton to the Fleet Air Arm Museum,' he said to Tiago. 'Shall we go there today, Tim?

Now I can drive again we can get there easily and it would be a fun day out. What do you think?'

'That sounds really cool,' Tiago replied, cheering up. He always loved to see the helicopters flying over to Portland and knew they had some in the museum.

They set off and were there within an hour. It was incredibly interesting and they both really enjoyed the day out. The cloud seemed to lift from Tiago's mind and he was laughing and enjoying himself. They stayed until almost closing time and then began the drive back to Weymouth. On the way they were surprised to see lots of police cars parked in a layby and a little further down the road they were stopped by a police roadblock. They wondered what was happening when the police, very politely, asked them to get out and to open the boot of the car. A police dog was sniffing around it, too.

'That's fine. Don't look so worried, young man,' the police officer said to Tiago. 'We're searching for an escaped prisoner. He won't get far, but it may be a set-up job and so we stop and search every vehicle. On you go, and sorry to disturb your journey.'

It did disturb Tiago. Prisons and prisoners reminded him of his mum and her sad death, and of Jack. He presumed that by now the trial had taken place and he was in some prison, somewhere. He hoped he was locked up safely. There were several prisons in the area and at times he saw the large vans which transported prisoners from one prison to another being driven from the Portland prison. They were so distinctive with their small windows placed high up in the van.

Mr P appeared to notice the cloud of depression was descending again on Tiago and so talked about the incident.

'You can't worry about what happened to Jack. I'm sure you're quite safe and he will be in prison miles from here. Put it out of your mind. I thought we would take the back road from Dorchester and call at the farm. Even though we were delayed by the search, it's not too late and we haven't seen Dan and Daisy since they arrived back in Dorset.'

'That's a great idea, I'd forgotten they were coming back a bit sooner as the weather was getting cold.'

It was the first time that Tiago had visited the farmhouse since he ran away after the murder victim had been found. Shep heard them pull up and ran to the gate and covered him with licks. The commotion brought Dan and Daisy out of the vardo and Sandy appeared as well. There was such excitement at the reunion! It was just what was needed and soon they were all talking and laughing and drinking tea together. As usual, Daisy had a big pot of stew cooking and they were invited to stay for supper.

'Can I go up on the hill and see the sheep before it gets completely dark?' asked Tiago.

'Off you go, and take Shep with you, but don't be too long – supper's almost ready,' said Dan.

Even though it was nearly dark, Tiago knew his way up the hill so well he didn't stumble. Shep was by his side and he loved seeing the sheep again. Some were this year's lambs and didn't know him, but the older ewes nuzzled up to him. They were quite large, owing to being pregnant. He knew that the Dorset sheep, because of the very mild climate, gave birth to autumn and winter lambs. Then he and Shep raced down the hill together, just as they had when they worked together. It almost didn't seem possible that only a year had passed since he'd run away from London; so much had happened, and he had such a good life now.

Supper was great, and throughout it Sandy sat on his lap and purred, a mature cat now.

'We'll see you again soon,' Mr P and Tiago promised as they waved goodbye. They drove down the road and into Weymouth, using the route that brought back so many memories. When they arrived home after such an eventful day, Mr P felt it was the right time to talk about another issue which he had been thinking about ever since they visited London.

'Even before you mother died I had been wondering how you might feel about adoption, and I know that Val told you that your mother had talked to the social worker and written a letter to say she would be happy for both her children to be adopted. I want you to know that I'd just love to have you as my son, not just my ward and foster son. I'll always protect you anyway, you know that, whatever decision you make, but adoption would give you a new name, a new identity and new start for adult life. I have spoken to my own few relatives about this and they are all happy. It wouldn't have made any difference even if they raised objections – for you've proved to be more than a son to me with all your kindness.

'I don't want an answer now; I want you to think about it. Adoption makes you my son forever. Also, you need to know that I'll understand completely if you say no – this must be your choice. When you have thought it through, just tell me your answer, and I'll love you and take care of you just the same, whatever that answer is. I have raised the issue now because these things take time and once you are eighteen, you are no longer a minor and there would be no need for adoption in the eyes of the law, so if you want me to adopt you, then I would start the legal process at once.'

Tiago was stunned by this proposal. His emotions were so raw at that moment that he could hardly speak. Mr P seemed to understand completely.

'Let's watch a film before we go to bed,' he suggested. 'Find something funny – we could do with a good laugh together.'

Mr P turned on the TV while Tiago went to choose a DVD. When he came back, the local news was being shown and it was featuring the incident on the A37 between Yeovil and Dorchester where a prisoner had absconded when the van had stopped for the driver to change a punctured tyre. A photo of the prisoner was shown, and viewers were told to be careful and contact the police if they saw anyone fitting the description, not to try to apprehend him themselves, as he could be violent.

Tiago screamed and dropped the DVD. He felt himself go pale and he began to shake all over.

'It's him – it's Jack,' he managed to say to Mr P. 'He can't be here in Dorset – he can't be on the run near us! Why didn't they put him in prison in some other place, miles away? He might see me around and he'd kill me, I know he would!'

'Tim,' said Mr P, calmly. 'Tim, he absconded near Yeovil – that's miles away, and he would have no idea you're living in Dorset, would he? Even if it was remotely possible that he did see you somewhere, he'd never recognise Tim Cox – the strong lad that you now are. You don't even speak like a Londoner any more; you have quite a Dorset accent now! You're living under my protection as my foster son and I have promised always to take care of you. Try to trust me, I will make sure no harm comes to you. I'll phone Mrs Jennings first thing in the morning and tell her your fears, but I am sure they are groundless. He's not likely to get far, anyway, and this breakout will add to his sentence. All will be well.'

Tiago tossed and turned that night. Next day, seeing he was still troubled, Mr P had a suggestion. 'Tim, why don't you go into the workshop and work on that rocking chair you're making for Zoe-Ann for Christmas? There's nothing like working with wood to soothe your feelings.'

Maybe Mr P was right, Tiago thought; working on Zoe-Ann's rocking chair might make him feel better. He put the heater on and began to sand down the arms. It was soothing but didn't take the bewilderment and inner pain away. He felt a huge urge to burn himself, to burn out the anguish he was feeling inside, but something in his brain warned him that if he began to self-harm again, it would be a slippery slope from which he would find it hard to escape – just like his mum with her drugs. As he thought about his mother, tears began to spill down his cheeks once again. He longed for Zoe-Ann to hold him, just as she had at the funeral. At that moment, she seemed very far away. He told himself to calm down before he phoned her; he was almost a grown man, he ought not to cry.

The rocking chair was almost finished – just the final sanding, oiling and polishing to do. It did look good and Tiago was proud of his work. He sat in the chair and began to rock himself gently. He thought of Mr P and how kind he had been. He had grown very fond of him and appreciated everything he had taught him. He wondered if it would make any difference if he were adopted as a legal son.

But Tiago was in turmoil. Part of him could hear the rhyme playing yet again like a recording in his mind – 'Run, run, as fast as you can!' – but where could he run? Not back to London and not back to Dan and Daisy. Did he really want to be on the run again, back living on the streets, with no hope and no future? His life had been so different in recent months, and in his heart of hearts he didn't want that to change. He sat for ten or so minutes just rocking to and fro, his mind full of confused thoughts.

Suddenly he was startled by the ringtone of his phone. He pulled it out of his pocket and looked at the number and it made his heart leap – Zoe-Ann was calling him.

'Hi, Zoe-Ann,' he answered. 'Are you OK? You don't usually phone this early on a Sunday. Haven't you gone to church?'

'We're having a late service today and lunch afterwards, so I thought I would phone you. I know it's silly,' she replied, 'but I just sensed inside that something isn't right and felt that I should call you early. Even if everything's fine, I just want to hear your voice again!'

For a moment Tiago was silent. How wonderful his girl was! Then he decided to tell her exactly what had happened and how he was feeling.

'Have you got time to listen?' he asked. 'I've got a lot on my mind.'

It did take quite a while to tell her all that had transpired the day before and to try to explain how confused he was now feeling. Zoe-Ann was a good listener. But he realised when he had finished that she was not sure what to say.

'Ti,' she said eventually, 'I'm not sure that I am the best person to help you. I don't want you to disappear and run away again, but as to advice about adoption, I can't do that. Dad's still in his study, do you think you could share your news with him? He can probably help more than me.'

Tiago agreed, so she took the phone to her dad, explaining just a little about his situation.

'Have you got plenty of battery life on your phone?' he asked Tiago, gently. 'This could take some time.'

'I'm in the workshop and time isn't a problem and my phone's battery's OK,' answered Tiago.

'Then tell me what has happened and how you feel about it all,' suggested Richard.

Tiago took a deep breath and plunged once again into an account of the previous day's happenings and all his confused feelings. It did take a while, especially because at times he needed to compose himself and stop the tears from flowing. Richard listened quietly, saying very little, but allowing Tiago to take the time he needed to express his emotions. Then he said, 'I've just a couple of thoughts to share with you, Tim – I want you to hear them knowing that I'm a dad, not just a vicar trying to counsel you. First, you need to decide if you are going to keep on running from difficult situations or if you are strong enough to face them. This decision might decide the pattern of your whole life – for if running away becomes your option every time you are struggling, then you may never have a normal, stable life. Have you got enough support to stand against the threat Jack poses to you, should it in fact materialise? If you run away again, will you always have him as a shadow over your shoulder, for he could turn up anywhere? That's the first big issue you need to decide. I can't tell you what to do – it's something you must think through.'

Richard paused for a few seconds and then continued, 'The other big issue is about fatherhood. I want to suggest that this is deeper than just the question of whether you are adopted by Mr P or not – because we both know that he loves you and will help you, whether you take his name or not and are legally his son. One day we all lose our parents; it's a fact of life that in due course death separates us, as you have sadly found out. What we humans need is an anchor for our drifting lives – and now I do talk as a vicar. God, our Creator, also longs to be our Father, our Friend through His Son, Jesus, someone who will never leave us, whatever happens to us in life. All you need to do is to ask Him to be your Father and grow a relationship with Him. When that issue is settled then we have a peace and stability within us, because we become the people we were created to be, and it changes life completely.

'So, these two things are suggestions for you to think about and decide for yourself. I will only add that I'm always willing to talk to you if you want more help or advice – any time of the day or night – not just because that's my job, but because you are special, not only to Zoe-Ann, but to our whole family and most of all, to God.'

'Thank you,' answered Tiago. 'I feel better for telling you my worries and I'll think about what you said. Thanks so much.'

chapter twenty-five

The chat with Richard had helped Tiago's mind to clear, and over the next two or three days he thought seriously about the issues he was facing in his life. The next Saturday he decided to go into Weymouth and visit the church again. He found the prayer space and sat quietly, glad that no one else was around. In his mind he spoke to God.

'God,' he said, 'if You are real and love everyone, I want You to be my forever Father and help me make good life choices. You helped me to forgive my mum; please help me now to forgive Jack for all he did to mess up my life, and thank You for the good friends I have. Amen.'

This prayer did make a difference, and gradually in the days that followed Tiago found the confusion was less and he no longer felt so much self-hate which he had always felt since Jack had abused him, and the need to self-harm rarely entered his mind. Soon, he was sure within himself that he did want to be adopted and become Mr P's son. When he told him, Mr P beamed with delight and gave him a hug. 'I'll set things in motion right away for you to become Timothy Petheron,' he said. 'Not that it makes any difference in my love and care for you – but it will help you have a better future, and I'm so proud that you will take my name.'

With these two major issues settled, Tiago felt much happier and began to look forward to his sixteenth birthday which was fast approaching, followed by Christmas.

The days went by very quickly. Tiago was working very hard at school, making up for the time he'd lost when he was living rough. He also continued making jewellery for the shop in Weymouth, and finishing his Christmas gifts for Zoe-Ann and Lizzie, and something he was making for Mr P, which was to be a surprise. This was a wooden box, with 'Dad' carved on the outside, and would be a place for him to keep his keys.

As well as working hard in the workshop, he had extra visits each week from Mrs Jennings about the adoption process, but she warned that it wouldn't happen in a hurry, because the courts always took their time. His only problem was trying to remember to call Mr P 'Dad' – but even that was getting easier.

Mr P had been delighted when Tiago had told him that he would like to be adopted. He had thrown himself into planning a party for Tiago's sixteenth birthday – hiring a hall, inviting Zoe-Ann and her family, as well as Dan and Daisy. He had invited Tom and Val to bring Lizzie, but knew that they were unlikely to make it, even though her health was improving. Tiago had invited some of his school friends to come with their girlfriends, and Mr P had asked Bob, Lorna and Guy Hall, and Mrs Jennings. A few of his close friends were also coming. He intended to announce to them at the party that Tiago had agreed to be his son. It was to be a celebration to remember!

Tiago's birthday fell on a Saturday that year, so it was an ideal day to hold the party. Mr P had arranged for the celebration to be held at a hotel – a very old manor house which overlooked the Fleet Lagoon and Chesil Beach. It was a family hotel, so it was a great place for Zoe-Ann's family to stay, as well as Mr P and Tiago. Even Dan and Daisy had decided to stay overnight, as their grandson was staying with them for the winter and could take care of things at the farm. The venue was just perfect, and the evening was dry and frosty, so the log fires in the old, large fireplaces were welcoming and homely. Tiago was overwhelmed.

He couldn't remember ever having a birthday party before. Zoe-Ann looked so beautiful in a new full-length blue dress and he was so proud to show her off to all his school friends.

'I told you my girl lives in London,' he said to his friends, as he introduced her. She was wearing the jewellery he had made for her and it was much admired.

'When Tim started coming to our school all of us girls wanted to catch his eye and we were a bit put out when he didn't respond,' Jade, one of his classmates, told Zoe-Ann. 'He's a great guy and we all like him.' Zoe-Ann chuckled and thought how different that was to the way his former classmates had treated him in Islington. She took several photos on her phone and thought she might show them round when she went back.

Zoe-Ann had no idea how much trouble those photos would cause.

The food, the music and dancing had been wonderful, and as the evening came to an end, Mr P stood up to make a short speech.

'I want not only to wish Tim a very happy sixteenth birthday, but to tell you all that he has agreed to be my adopted son. It will take a few months for the legalities to be completed, but when they are, his new name will be Timothy Petheron. Please raise your glasses to wish my son a very happy birthday and a happy future.'

After the toast had been drunk and a large birthday cake cut, Tiago and Zoe-Ann escaped onto the terrace. It was chilly, but Tiago put his arm around Zoe-Ann and drew her close to himself. The moon was shining on the dark sea and he sighed a deep sigh of happiness.

'I wish we could just stay here forever,' he said. 'I've never felt so happy in my entire life.'

Zoe-Ann snuggled close to him. 'I don't think I've ever felt so happy, either. Being here in this special place with you is wonderful. I don't want it to end.'

'I've made a little present for you,' Tiago said, handing her a package. Zoe-Ann looked at him, her eyes dancing in the moonlight. She tore the paper off the parcel and said 'Wow' when she saw a Welsh love spoon, beautifully carved from two pieces of wood – light and dark twisted together.

'Oh, Ti,' exclaimed Zoe-Ann. 'It's beautiful! I so love it. It's like my fair hair and your dark hair twisted together. I'll get Dad to put a hook above my bed, so that I can hang it up. How lucky I am to have you as my boyfriend!' She threw herself into his arms again and they kissed.

'Come inside and get warm by the fire,' he suggested. 'I must say goodbye to my guests.'

As he led her away from the terrace and into the hotel, he could see her eyes were glowing. No one had ever looked at him in the way she did at that moment. He felt he would burst with happiness!

The guests began to say goodbye and to go home. Zoe-Ann's mum sent the boys up to bed and Dan and Daisy decided to retire as well. Then, as they sat by the glowing embers, Zoe-Ann showed her parents and Mr P the beautiful present Tiago had made for her.

'I didn't know what to give you. I'm not clever at making things,' she explained to Tiago, 'but here is my present for you.'

Tiago took the beautifully wrapped package and began to open it.

'Oh, that's so cool,' he exclaimed as he opened a photobook. It had some photos of Zoe-Ann from her babyhood all through to the last summer holiday, which had lots of photos of the fun times they had together. 'I just love it, Zoe-Ann! I shall look at it every day. It's the best thing you could have given me. Thanks so much!'

Zoe-Ann was so pleased that he loved the book. It had been hard to think of something special for him, and then she had the idea of creating some special memories, as so many of Tiago's had been bad ones.

'I have a present, too,' said Mr P, handing an envelope to Tiago.

'But you've already given me this wonderful party,' said Tiago. 'I don't need any other present.'

'Open it and see, son,' Mr P suggested, and when he did, an airline ticket fell out.

'It's to go to Portugal!' exclaimed Tiago in surprise.

'Yes, Tim,' explained Mr P. 'I thought you and I would go to Portugal for the Christmas holidays and try to find your relatives. Now, I think it's well past all our bedtimes,' Mr P commented, 'You and Zoe-Ann had better say your goodnights and I want to have a quick chat to Richard and Jo about taking Lizzie's doll's cot and something else back to London,' he added, with a wink. The adults walked off to the bar and the two youngsters made their way upstairs, holding hands.

'This is the best birthday I have ever had,' Tiago whispered to Zoe-Ann, as he gently kissed her goodnight.

chapter twenty-six

Jack had planned his escape very carefully from the time he had been informed that he was to be transferred from the Midlands down to a prison in the West Country. His prison experience was bad, since it soon got around that he was a sex offender. He had plenty of contacts outside and it was surprisingly easy to still get drugs and deal them inside. Even drones were used sometimes – it was amazing what could be obtained for the right price. He had learned all sorts of things when driving lorries from one end of Europe to the other, even smuggling migrants into the country and evading the border patrols and Customs and Excise people, all experience which now stood him in good stead. He had managed to tamper with one of the tyres of the prison van, even while handcuffed to a prison officer, and roughly timed how long it would be before it punctured. When it did, they pulled into a layby and it couldn't have been more perfect!

'While you change that tyre, I really need a comfort stop very urgently,' he had told the officer to whom he was padlocked. They had made their way into the trees and the instant his padlock was undone, he dealt a blow to the officer which incapacitated him for several minutes, during which time he was gone, thanking his lucky stars that it was late afternoon and he was in some woods. He was well on his way before any search was organised by the local police force – the middle of the countryside was good for that. As soon as he thought it was safe enough, he stripped off his prison garb and hid it, as he was wearing his football kit underneath, which he had managed to filch after a game at the prison. Nobody had noticed he looked a bit fatter when he was put into the van!

Jack started to make his way north. He guessed there would be police patrols set up on the major roads and so kept to lanes for a long time. Passing through a village he noticed a car parked by the side of the road. It had quite an old registration number, and Jack thought he would be able to get into it without too much trouble and get it to start. His early years training as a car mechanic had taught him a few tricks and within minutes he had started the engine, and took off at speed. He also found some money in the glove compartment. He drove for a while and found himself in a small town. Noticing the sign to a railway station, he abandoned the car in a side street, entered the station and waited for the next train which was scheduled to stop at several major towns. Using several trains, he made his way to London, where he had contacts and places where he could hide out.

Jack was ready to escape to Europe, laughing to himself that he could travel in the same way as the migrants had travelled into the UK, but first he wanted to get even with somebody. He knew it was risky, but hate consumed him whenever he thought of Tiago and how he grassed on him and got him sent to prison, and he wanted to fix the kid once and for all. First, he needed to find out where he was now living. He guessed that someone in Islington would know. He was sly and devious, and hate gave him an energy which drove him. He had people who owed him, he had supplied them with drugs and they were under his thumb – he would find out in time what he wanted to know.

Jack waited in a safe hideout for a while, growing a full beard to try to disguise himself. Then he began to wander in the street market where Tiago had worked, listening to conversations, hoping by chance he might get some information. He was getting frustrated because he was learning nothing, when one evening there was a knock at the door.

As his mate, who owned the property, went to answer it, Jack disappeared into the cellar and into a cupboard where he could hide in case the cops came calling.

'It's OK, Jack,' his mate called to him. 'Come up, it's one of my contacts and he has news for you.'

Jack climbed the stairs, his heart thumping. People rarely came to the house and he was always scared when they did.

'Hi, mate,' a youngish man greeted him. 'I hear you are looking for that lad who ran away from the high school in Islington a year or so ago. My daughter was talking about him at teatime. One of her classmates went to his birthday party – she showed her some photos. He lives outside Weymouth, somewhere near sea in a caravan with a woodwork workshop. He makes wooden jewellery – the girl showed my daughter a bracelet he'd made her. Can't tell you any more, but thought you'd be interested in what I found out.'

'Sure thing,' answered Jack, with a grin. 'Very helpful, mate. I'll reward you for your work. I just want to see my stepson again, make sure he's doing alright. Thanks. Let's a have drink together before you go.'

Jack had enough information – soon he would make a plan.

After the birthday party, time passed very quickly to the end of term. Mr P obtained a passport for Tiago; with permission from social services, all their plans were laid to go to Portugal for two weeks. As the time drew closer, Tiago became more and more excited. He and Mr P made a file of all they knew about his father and his grandparents, and Tiago had borrowed travel guides from the library and read them from cover to cover. His only sadness was that Zoe-Ann wasn't coming with them; that would have made the adventure perfect, but he promised to keep in touch every day. They set up an app on their phones, so that they could 'chat' online easily.

It was a crisp, bright December day when they left to go to Gatwick Airport. Tiago was like a small child, he was so excited. He had never been to an airport before, let alone flown in a plane; so all the hanging around, getting through security, and so on, didn't bother him at all.

Once they had boarded, he sat by the window, his nose against the glass. There was no way he was going to miss seeing everything he could! Once they were at altitude above the clouds, he settled to read. The flight took two and a half hours and it seemed no time at all before the pilot announced they were making their descent to land at Porto Airport. When they entered the arrivals lounge, they saw a guy holding up a card with Mr P's name. He had come from the hotel to collect them. The journey into the city took about a quarter of an hour, but by now the sun had set and it was difficult to see very much. They would have to wait until the following day to explore.

The hotel was decorated for Christmas and almost all of the staff spoke good English, welcoming Mr P and Tiago warmly. Tiago was so glad to learn that he didn't have to order food in Portuguese, and that there was fish and chips on the menu, his favourite meal!

The next day was dry and bright – a perfect day to explore Porto. They planned to make investigations about his family and how to get to Braga, the last known address of his paternal grandparents. Tiago had decided that he must look like the locals since people began to greet him in Portuguese, whereas they used English for Mr P. He quickly began to pick up a few words.

Mr P had done some research and so as well as sightseeing, they went to a public office and asked about trying to connect with Tiago's relatives. It was amazing how helpful everyone was, especially when they heard the story of his father dying at sea when he was only a young boy. They were given a few leads to follow up in Braga and were told that it was quick and easy to reach the town by train, leaving from the São Bento station.

The pair decided to do that the following day. Meanwhile, they went to the waterfront of the river Douro and found a café where they could have lunch and enjoy watching the boats go up and down. The other side of the river was a twin town, Vila Nova de Gaia, where they could see the advertisements for the many port wine lodges. A beautiful bridge connected the two. On the river were some old barges, such as were used to transport the port wine down the Douro River to the lodges years ago. There were so many interesting things to see and learn about, Tiago wished they could stay for a long time and see everything. However, it was December and the days were short, so after lunch they had a ride on a very old-fashioned tram to the tram museum and enjoyed looking around. The museum curator chatted to them.

'We don't have many visitors during the winter,' he commented. 'Most British people like to go to the Algarve and enjoy the warmth. Here it is often wet – we have more rain here than you do in Manchester!'

'Really?' questioned Tiago. 'I thought Portugal was warm and sunny.'

'Not up here in the north, and we get many gales in the winter with the sea coming right over the esplanade at times. However, it is a good place to visit for Christmas. You must try our speciality, *bacalhau*. That is a favourite food for Christmas dinner.'

'What is *bacalhau* like? I've never heard of it,' said Tiago.

'It is dried and salted codfish,' the curator answered. 'Everyone loves it.'

'Oh', said Tiago, not wanting to be rude, but it sounded horrible to him.

'There is something very British happening this evening,' the guy went on to tell them. 'There's an English church here, just above the Crystal Palace park, and tonight at nine o'clock they have carols by candlelight and then mince pies afterwards. I have English friends who always go and sometimes I go along as well. I'll draw you a map, if you like. It's not difficult to find.'

Tiago looked at Mr P, who nodded and said, 'Yes, please, that sounds like a lovely idea. We can get a taxi from the hotel after dinner.'

As the curator drew the map he warned them that the church was hidden. It had to be entered through a door in a high wall – that was from past history, as when it was built in Georgian times it was illegal to have a Protestant church in the city. However, the many port wine lodge owners had petitioned for an Anglican place of worship, and this compromise had been reached.

'Can we go?' asked Tiago, eagerly. 'I just love singing carols – it would be a proper start to Christmas. Who knows – someone might know about my family!'

chapter twenty-seven

After dinner that evening, Mr P and Tiago went by taxi to find the 'English' church. It was indeed behind a tall wall, but once they had entered the gate, they gasped with surprise. Around the church was a garden, all lit up with fairy lights. It looked beautiful! Inside the church, they were welcomed and given candles to hold, as the service was to be by candlelight. Everyone seemed very friendly. Tiago was quiet for a moment and asked God to help him find his Portuguese family.

They both enjoyed singing all the traditional carols and hearing the lessons read, and afterwards were invited into a hall behind the church to have mince pies and mulled wine and fruit punch. A young man came over to Tiago and greeted him.

'Hello, Antonio, I didn't expect to see you here. I thought you had gone home for the school holidays.'

Tiago said, 'I'm sorry, but you must have the wrong person. My name's Tiago Costa, and I live in England.'

'Sorry, Tiago, I'm a teacher at one of the international schools here and you are the spitting image of one of my pupils. I'm Mark Watson. Did you say your surname was Costa?' Tiago nodded, and Mark looked thoughtful for a moment. 'The strange thing is that the lad in my class, Antonio, is also called Costa. It's quite a common name over here, but you look so alike, it's almost as if you are his double.'

'Actually, I am over here to try to find some of my dad's relatives.' Tiago explained. 'If I look so like this boy, maybe we could be related.'

'I could contact his father on the off-chance that he might know something about your lost family. Can you tell me more?'

Mr P explained the situation to Mark and gave him the scant information that they had, and said, 'It seems so unlikely, but who knows? If you can contact them without causing any inconvenience, then we'd be very grateful, thank you, because we don't know where to begin our search.'

'OK, I'll have to go outside to make a couple of phone calls, because of the reception here. Antonio's father works at the sports club, and I have the number for there. Even if he's off-duty, they will give me his personal number, I'm sure, if I explain the situation.'

Mark went outside the hall to make the calls. Meanwhile, Tiago and Mr P ate their mince pies, thinking how incredible it would be if this boy was, indeed, a relative.

They only had a short while to wait, for Mark came in and smiled at them. 'There is a connection. I knew it – the likeness between the boys is unmistakable! I chatted to Antonio's father. He said his brother married an Englishwoman and they lived in London, and he was drowned in a fishing accident years ago and they lost contact with the wife, who had a baby boy.'

'That was me! He must be my uncle, though I didn't know I had one; I only had the names of my grandparents. Amazing! This is so cool – we've found one of my relatives,' Tiago said in excitement. 'So this Antonio, he must be my cousin.'

'You'll soon know because Mr Costa wants to talk to you – it's been a shock to him to hear about his brother after all these years, but he wants to see his nephew and guardian. I'll punch in the numbers. It's easier to talk outside. Don't worry, he speaks good English!' added Mark, handing the phone to Mr P.

Outside it was quiet. They spoke to Tiago's uncle, and answered his questions. He told them that Tiago's grandparents were still alive, but no longer lived in Braga. They had retired and moved and bought a house on the coast at Aveiro.

'Where are you staying?' he asked Mr P, who told them the name of the hotel. 'I know it,' he answered. 'Could we meet up tomorrow? It's my day off, so I could bring my wife and sons to meet you. I'll explain to my parents we have met. It will be a big shock to them and they will need time to get used to the idea that they have another grandson. They only speak a few words of English, so it won't be easy to communicate. Let me talk to them first then arrange a time when I can take you to visit.'

Tiago marvelled. He had asked God to help him find his family, and already he had an answer. It was truly amazing – a sort of Christmas miracle. They thanked Mark so much, glad that he had spoken to them and mistaken Tiago for his cousin, and then been kind enough to make the contact.

That night, although Tiago tried to sleep, he was so excited that his mind kept working and he was thinking all the time about having grandparents and uncles, aunts and cousins. He hoped some of them would speak good English. He finally dropped off to sleep just as it was beginning to get light and woke with a start when his alarm sounded.

This was the day when he would meet some of his family! After breakfast when they were due to arrive, he suddenly felt very shy. What if they didn't like him? His life's history wasn't very good. His head was in a spin and he had so many questions that he hoped would be answered.

Waiting in the hotel lounge to meet his relatives, he began to message Zoe-Ann and tell her the extraordinary news. He pressed 'send' and looked up to see a family coming through the main door of the hotel. The family rushed towards him and Mr P and were soon laughing, crying and hugging them. It felt very strange – not at all English!

There were three boys. Antonio was the eldest, and he did look almost as if he could be Tiago's twin! There was a strong family resemblance. He was fourteen. Then he was introduced to Ricardo, who was twelve, and Petra, who was ten. The boys were very excited to find a long-lost cousin. His aunt and uncle began to ask questions – how was his mother? Did he have any brothers or sisters? Where did he live? The questions were endless. They ordered coffee for the adults and cold drinks for the kids and lovely sweet little cakes, which were dripping with honey and very delicious. Even though Tiago had not long eaten a good breakfast he couldn't resist tasting a few.

'We've had a bit of a bad time, lately,' Tiago answered. 'My mum was sick for quite a long time and finally went into hospital and then the hospice, where she died recently. By that time, Lizzie was being looked after by some very good friends, who are now her foster parents. She still lives in Islington, and has been very ill, too, with leukaemia, but now with my stem cells, is getting better. I left London and went to live with Mr P, who's my legal guardian and my foster dad. We live by the sea in a town called Weymouth. It's a long way from London, but I love it there.'

The questions kept coming, and when they started to ask about Lizzie's father and where he was, Mr P took over, seeing that Tiago was getting a bit agitated, explaining to the family that they didn't know exactly where he was living, since he deserted the family before their mother became so ill. Tiago was grateful. Mr P knew exactly how to answer the questions without telling lies, but without giving away bad family secrets.

Soon, the conversation changed, and they were making plans for Christmas Day. Traditionally in Portugal, Christmas is celebrated and gifts exchanged on Christmas Eve, but his uncle and aunt had spread the good news of Tiago coming to find his family and everyone had been invited to the grandparents' home in Aveiro to meet him on Christmas Day.

'Your visit will make Christmas even more special this year. We'll come and collect you on Christmas morning, straight after breakfast,' suggested Tiago's uncle. 'We'll probably stay until late in the evening. Be prepared to meet lots more relatives. We're a big family and everyone is excited about meeting you!'

'That will be amazing,' Tiago said. 'I didn't know I had a big family. I've never known any grandparents, either, so I'm well excited about meeting them. I want to go shopping today and buy them a present. What do you think they will like?'

'Your grandmother loves flowers,' his uncle told him, 'and your granddad is a chocoholic – I think that's what you call it in English – he adores chocolate.'

'Thanks, I want to buy them something they'll really like,' he answered. Then his uncle, aunt and cousins left, leaving them to shop. The next day was Christmas Eve and they wanted to have their shopping finished before then, so that they could enjoy that day together then have Christmas Day with all the family.

chapter twenty-eight

The night of 23rd December, unbeknown to Tiago and Mr P, terrible things were about to happen back at their home.

At Tiago's birthday party, Mr P had asked a favour of Daisy and Dan. He was planning a surprise homecoming for Tiago – a move from the draughty old caravan back into the main house. It hadn't been lived in since Mr P's wife had died, although he had spring cleaned it from time to time. Now, partly on the advice of social services, he was going to live in it again.

'I just wondered,' he had said to Dan and Daisy, 'if there is any possibility that you could help me get the surprise ready? You're welcome to live in the house while we're away, and if you could move in some of our belongings so that it would look homely when we got back, that would be amazing.'

'What a grand idea,' Daisy had answered at once. 'Our grandson will drive us down, I'm sure, and he'll stay and look after the sheep up at the farm. He's planning on staying with us over the winter this year, just like Tim did last year. He'll help move some of your stuff, too, I don't doubt. He's a real good lad, just like your Tim. He's got his own dog, so we can bring Shep down to keep us company.'

So, the arrangement was made. Noah, their grandson, was very helpful and moved most of the furniture with Dan, while Daisy began to spring clean the house.

'This is just the weather I need to give this house a good clean,' Daisy told Dan and Noah. 'The curtains and rugs can have a good airing in the east wind, and it's nice and sunny, too.'

'I'll give you a hand with anything else you need done,' said Noah. 'We've nearly finished moving all the gear in. Don't forget I'm coming down for Christmas dinner, too,' he added with a cheeky grin.

By the evening of 23rd December, they had everything ready and the house looked bright and cheery. Daisy had even found a box of decorations and put some up. It had been hard work and Dan and Daisy were tired. Within minutes of going to bed, they fell asleep. Around 2am Dan stirred, and was surprised to find Shep tugging at the bed clothes.

'What is it, boy?' he said. 'You want to go out?' As he got out of bed, he thought he heard a noise. Shep's ears were up and he barked.

'Quiet, Shep, lie,' he said, as he crept over to the window and looked out. The moonlight allowed him to see the shadow of a person, near the caravan. Within seconds he pulled on his trousers and a sweater, reached for his mobile to use as a torch, and went downstairs, Shep at his heels.

'Wish I had my shotgun,' Dan said to himself. 'That would scare any prowler off!'

He pulled back the bolts, grateful that he'd oiled them that morning. Reminding Shep to stay quiet and sit at the open door, he looked out. The bright moonlight enabled him to see clearly and he was horrified. The intruder had a can and was pouring the fluid from it around the caravan. This was no wandering tramp – it was arson!

His instinctive thought that he would be blamed just because he was a Romany made him quickly take a photo of the guy, before he rushed over, calling Shep to follow, but he was too late to stop the blaze, which had already been started.

Within seconds the place was on fire, flames leaping high into the sky. The smell reached his throat and the smoke stung his eyes as he reached again for his phone and dialled 999. It seemed liked hours before the call was answered, and he gave details of what was happening. It could only have been seconds, but by now the whole caravan was ablaze.

Dan sent Shep to get the man, while he struggled through the thick smoke, aware of the intense heat as he made his way over the yard, stumbling over the rough stones and trying not to fall. The arsonist was startled by Shep, who had begun to bark loudly and then grabbed his trouser leg. In spite of the dog's natural fear of fire, he hung on to his quarry.

'Come on – come on, where are you?' Dan muttered to himself, looking in the direction of the lane and hoping the fire brigade would soon arrive. Then he saw Daisy struggling to join him, with a hosepipe from the workshop.

'Get away, love,' he called. 'Caravan's beyond saving. Douse the wood around the workshop, maybe you can save that.' Then he heard a huge bang and explosion coming from inside the caravan. The noise and smoke were terrifying, and Dan knew he was becoming disorientated. Every now and then he glanced down the drive to see if the fire engine was coming – it seemed to be taking so long.

'Shep, come here,' he called, but Shep was still holding on to the trousers of the intruder, who with a sudden lurch tried to free himself from the dog and make his escape. But in doing so, he tripped and fell into the blaze.

Dan rushed forward, hoping to get the man and pull him to safety. The flames and smoke drove him back, but he put a hanky over his face and tried again. Dizziness came over him and he had to stumble back. Then at long last, he heard the sound of the fire engine arriving, and with it, an ambulance and an ambulance car.

'Over there, over there,' Dan called. 'A man has fallen over there into the fire!'

'It's OK, old man!' A large fireman came over and supported Dan just as he was falling. 'We're onto it.'

'Daisy, my Daisy is somewhere,' Dan said, not really remembering where she was or what she was doing. 'You must help my Daisy.'

'I'm here, Dan,' she shouted, running over. 'You alright?'

'Bit shaken up – but dread to think how that guy is. I tried, but I couldn't get to him. The smoke was in my eyes and choking me. Thought I was going to faint and fall in, too. Where's Shep?' he suddenly asked.

'He's OK, he's with me, came to me when I called him,' Daisy reassured him.

'You both need checking over – let's get you to the ambulance,' the fireman said, gently guiding Dan towards the vehicle.

In the other ambulance, paramedics were working on the man pulled from the fire. They took him to the hospital as soon as he was stable enough to move. Dan had some burns to his hands, but it was the smoke inhalation that was concerning the paramedic most of all.

'I think we need to take your husband to the hospital, too,' he told Daisy. 'Do you want to lock up the house and come along with us? Do you need to contact anyone?'

'I'll put Shep in the house and lock the door. I'll phone our grandson when we're at the hospital and let him know what's happened. Everything will be safe here, won't it? We were looking after it all for our friends. Oh, we must let them know,' Daisy said, distractedly.

Soon they were at the hospital and Dan was improving. When his burns had been treated and he was well enough, the police came to ask questions about how the fire had started, and he told them as best he could, showing them the photo on the phone.

Noah came to collect Daisy. He took her back to the house and stayed with her, since Dan needed to remain on a ward at least until the following afternoon. They were told that the arsonist was the escaped prisoner for whom the police had been searching for weeks. He was very badly burnt and needed to be transferred by air ambulance to a specialist hospital.

'Seems he was targeting the caravan for some reason,' the policeman told them when he came to take a proper statement. 'What a blessing that the owners were out of the country, or we might be investigating murder. At least only the caravan was destroyed – amazing that the workshop didn't catch fire, but I understand, Mrs Smith, that you did a good job of dousing around it. Well done! Now I hope you can rest easy and recover and try to enjoy Christmas.'

Everything smelt of smoke and all Dan's hard work of cleaning the outside of the windows had to be done again – but it was such a relief that neither the workshop nor the house were damaged.

'Thank goodness we had moved all their gear over before that happened,' Dan said, 'but now I need to speak to Mr P.'

'I'll get him on the phone, Granddad,' Noah promised, 'but the police have already been in touch and informed him. Just rest and I'll look after you both.'

chapter twenty-nine

Mr P woke with a start and looked at his bedside clock. 'Who on earth is ringing me at this unearthly hour of the morning?' he thought to himself, as he pressed the button to answer.

'Mr Petheron?' the voice asked, 'Sergeant Hughes here of the Dorset Police. I'm sorry to phone so early, but I have some bad news for you.' The policeman paused for a moment and Mr P wondered what on earth had happened. He only had distant relatives, and no one would bother to find him in Portugal in the early hours to tell him if one of them had died.

'It's about your home. Last night there was a fire in your caravan, destroying it completely. It appears to have been an arson attack and the suspect is in hospital with severe burns, under police guard. I'm not at liberty to tell you anything other than that he is an escaped prisoner for whom we have been searching the area for weeks now. Your workshop and house are undamaged. Your house-sitters did all they could. Mrs Smith is unharmed. Mr Smith suffered smoke inhalation and burns to his hands, but has been released from hospital and is recovering at home. We are sorry to convey such bad news at Christmas and will give you all the details when you return.'

'Thank you,' mumbled Mr P, and put the phone down. He was quite shaken. It wasn't that he was upset about the caravan; it had served its purpose. Anyway, the insurance would cover any loss. It was the thought that he and his foster son had been the intended victims in an arson attack, and possibly attempted murder. Thank God they were in Portugal. The prisoner the police had been looking for – it must have been Jack. How would he tell that to his son?

Mr P decided that he could not and would not spoil the boy's Christmas. This news could wait until Boxing Day. There was to be more than enough emotional turmoil to be faced in the next couple of days. Dan and Daisy were fine, so the rest of the news could wait. But he decided to ring Daisy before Tiago woke up. As it happened, Noah rang him first, and told him everything.

When Tiago woke, he felt so excited. It was Christmas Eve and he and Mr P had the whole day to go exploring the city.

There was a lovely breakfast at the hotel, but Tiago just didn't feel like eating – he was too excited. He thought Mr P seemed unusually quiet and noticed he didn't eat much. Tiago was surprised; then he wondered if his foster dad was worried that the grandparents would take him away from him? Could they do that? Would he become Portuguese, not British? Suddenly many worrying thoughts passed through his mind.

'Are you worried about me meeting my grandparents?' he asked Mr P. 'They won't be allowed to take me away from you, will they?'

'That thought never entered my head,' answered Mr P, with a smile. 'No, I was thinking about home. I always miss the Fleet and Weymouth when I go away, even though it's nice to visit new places. Let's finish breakfast and we can do some sightseeing in Porto. You'd better take lots of photos to show Zoe-Ann. Are you going to phone her this evening? Tomorrow it might not be so easy when we're with your family.'

They set out, and even the grey skies and occasional light drizzle didn't spoil their enjoyment of walking along the Douro River waterfront. There were little cafés where they could stop and have hot drinks when they felt tired. Everywhere looked bright and festive. In the afternoon they went for a short trip down the river on a pleasure boat. It was fun, but for Tiago the day did seem to drag. His mind kept wandering and thinking about whether his new-found family would like him. It was all so exciting, but scary, too.

They were eating hot, buttered toast in a café when Tiago felt his phone vibrate and he looked at the number – it was Zoe-Ann. He excused himself and went outside to take the call.

'Have you heard the news about your caravan?' Zoe-Ann's voice sounded worried.

'No, what about it?' questioned Tiago. Why would he hear about the caravan? It didn't make sense.

'I'm not sure what to say, but it was on the news this evening. They didn't say who owned the caravan, just that the owner was away, and it was burnt down during the night in an arson attack by an escaped prisoner. When I saw the pictures, I could see it was where you lived. I think it was on the London news because the prisoner was a man from Islington. I guessed he might be Jack.'

'Jack, it must be Jack, trying to kill me!' Tiago yelled down the phone. 'How can I tell Mr P? All his things burnt down! Oh, I hope the workshop and the machines are safe. They mean so much to him. Oh, Zoe-Ann – this awful news, and I was just going to ring you to tell you about finding my family! That can wait for now. I must tell Mr P. I've brought him nothing but trouble! I'll ring you back when I've told him.'

By the expression on his face, Tiago could see Mr P realised something was very wrong when he went back into the restaurant.

'What's up, son?' he asked. 'You look very upset.'

'Oh, Mr P – Dad,' Tiago said, struggling not to cry. 'The most terrible thing has happened. I just bring trouble wherever I go. Your caravan has been burnt down and it seems like Jack did it to get back at me. He said he would kill me if I ever grassed him up about abusing me. It was on the telly. Zoe-Ann has just rung me. She saw it on the news – our caravan was burnt down by an escaped prisoner! It *must* have been Jack. Oh, I'm so sorry! What trouble I've brought you – you took me in and look what's happened.'

'I know all about it, Tim,' said Mr P, calmly. 'The police rang me. I didn't tell you because I wanted these few days to be special for you. It's not as bad as you think. I had planned a surprise for you – when we go home we are going to be living in the house. I had asked Dan and Daisy to come over and live in the house and get it ready while we are over here, and take our personal possessions to it from the caravan. I have spoken to their grandson, and they are alright.

'They had already moved our things over and had gone to bed when Shep heard a noise. Dan investigated and saw a man pouring petrol around the caravan. He even got a shot of him on his phone before he phoned for the emergency services. Shep went for the man's trousers and I'm not quite sure what happened but the gas cylinder blew up and Jack is badly burnt and in hospital. Dan has minor injuries and Daisy saved the workshop by dousing it with the hose.' He smiled at his foster son. 'That's about as much as the police told me. We could have lost so much more. The old caravan was insured anyway. It's time I forgot the ghosts of the past and moved back into the house. I couldn't bear living there alone after my dear wife died. I knew it was time to move back with my new son – I'd just kept it as a surprise for you when we got home. Don't give the caravan another thought. You have brought me only joy and I'm so proud of my son!

'You had better get back on the phone to young Zoe-Ann and reassure her that all is well. Oh, and another reason for using the house again is so that we can have guests to stay – like Zoe-Ann and her family, Lizzie and hers and maybe your Portuguese family, too!'

'But what about Jack?'

'We don't know yet – he sounds badly injured. The police will make sure he is never a threat to you again.'

'Then it's a sort of new start for us all,' remarked Tiago, smudging his tears away.

'Yes, Tim, it really is, and I think we will have great times together,' replied Mr P.

Tiago took a deep breath and felt the tension go from his shoulders. It was so amazing to know that Mr P, his new dad, cared for him so deeply and didn't blame him for everything. As he stood looking at him, the old rhyme once again ran through his mind: 'Run, run, as fast as you can!' And he knew, suddenly, that he would never have to worry about that again.

'Hi, Zoe-Ann!' Tiago said, when he rang her back. 'Don't worry, it's all cool!' Then he explained the whole story. 'Just thank God that Dan and Daisy are OK and the police will never let Jack hurt me again. Tomorrow we're going to spend Christmas Day with my grandparents, uncles, aunts and cousins – there are a lot of them – so I might not get to talk to you. Have an amazing Christmas. I hope you like your present. It comes with my love.'

The little seaside fishing town of Aveiro looked beautiful the next morning, as Tiago's uncle drove them along the shoreline to see all the little painted houses. They were so quaint, and sparkled under the blue sky and sunshine of the cold, clear Christmas morning. Then they turned into a side road and drove up to a large house. Uncle beeped the horn and the house's front door opened. Tiago got out of the car feeling shy and a bit scared, but was immediately enveloped by his grandparents, quickly followed by uncles, aunts and cousins. A home-made banner hung over the door: 'Welcome home to Portugal, Tiago.'

A warm glow spread through his body and a huge smile came over his face – he had found his father's family and they were pleased to see him. He had discovered his Portuguese roots and felt that his life was falling into place at last. He had a new father in Mr P, a new home at Weymouth and now a new family in Portugal, and would never need to run again.